Table of CONTENTS

Introducing 4

Chapter 1
My Early Home 6

Chapter 2
Birtwick Park. 14

Chapter 3
Earlshall Park. 28

Chapter 4
A London Cab Horse. 44

Chapter 5
The Final Sale 56

INTRODUCING . . .

Duchess

Black Beauty's mother

Ginger

Black Beauty's carriage partner
and friend at Birtwick Park.

Jerry

A cabbie who owns
Black Beauty

Black BEAUTY

by Anna Sewell   retold by L. L. Owens   illustrated by Jennifer Tanner

Librarian Reviewer
Allyson A.W. Lyga MS
Library Media/Graphic Novel Consultant
Fulbright Memorial Fund Scholar, author

Reading Consultant
Mark DeYoung
Classroom Teacher, Edina Public Schools, MN
BA in Elementary Education, Central College
MS in Curriculum & Instruction, University of Minnesota

Graphic Revolve is published by Stone Arch Books,
A Capstone Imprint
151 Good Counsel Drive, P.O. Box 669
Mankato, Minnesota 56002
www.capstonepub.com

Library of Congress Cataloging-in-Publication Data
Owens, L. L.
    Black Beauty / by Anna Sewell; retold by L.L. Owens; illustrated by Jennifer
Tanner.
        p. cm.—(Graphic Revolve)
    ISBN-13: 978-1-59889-046-4 (library binding)
    ISBN-10: 1-59889-046-8 (library binding)
    ISBN-13: 978-1-59889-217-8 (paperback)
    ISBN-10: 1-59889-217-7 (paperback)
    1. Graphic novels. I. Tanner, Jennifer. II. Sewell, Anna, 1820-1878. Black
Beauty. III. Title. IV. Series.
PN6727.O985B63 2007
741.5'973—dc22   2006007691

Summary: Black Beauty grows up in the fields and horse meadows of Victorian
England. His peaceful childhood fades away as he faces human cruelty and
mistreatment in a world that cares little for the happiness of animals.

Credits
Art Director: Heather Kindseth
Graphic Designer: Kay Fraser

Printed in the United States of America in Stevens Point, Wisconsin.
102012
006968R

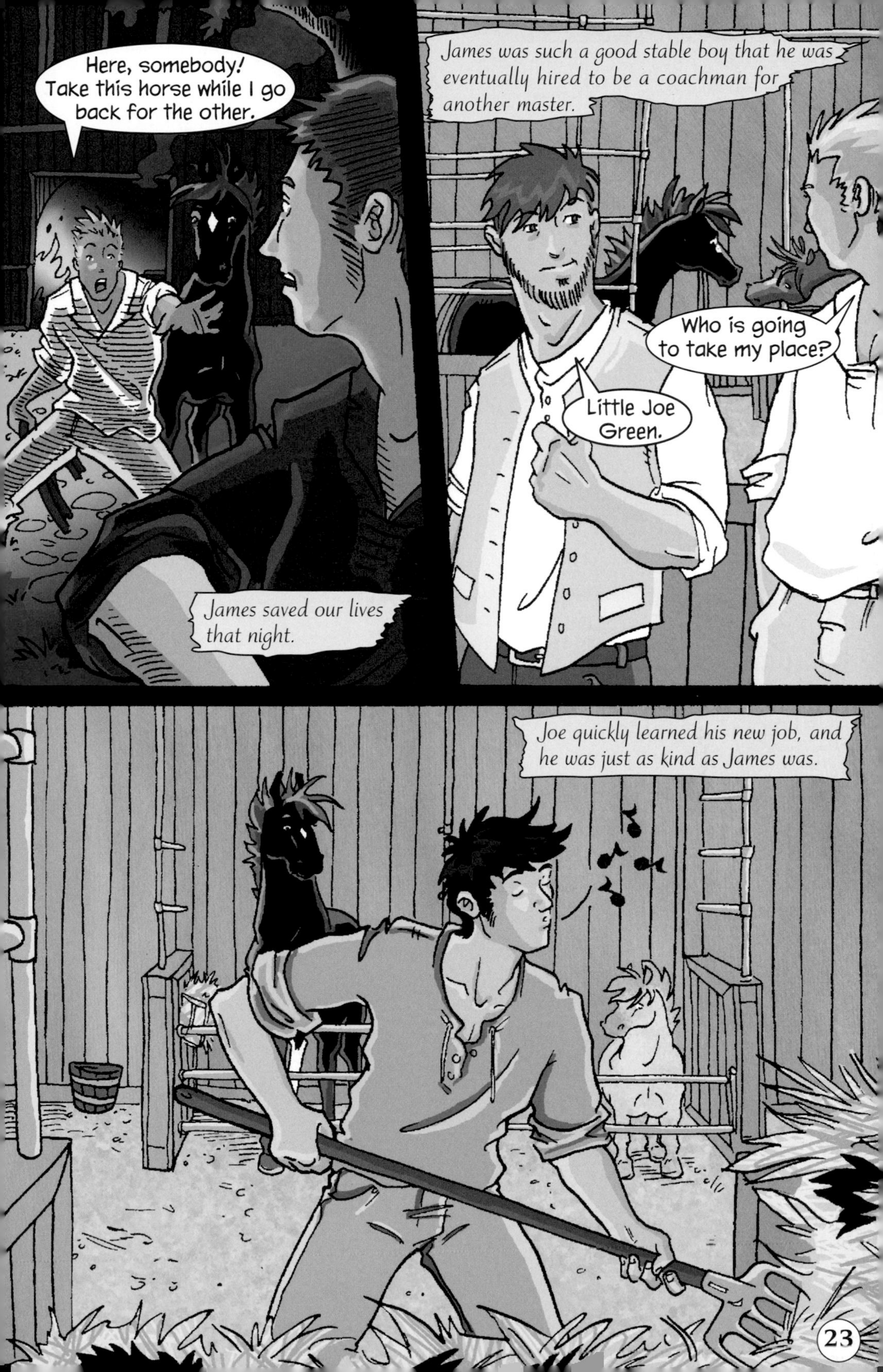

Here, somebody! Take this horse while I go back for the other.
James saved our lives that night.
James was such a good stable boy that he was eventually hired to be a coachman for another master.
Who is going to take my place?
Little Joe Green.
Joe quickly learned his new job, and he was just as kind as James was.

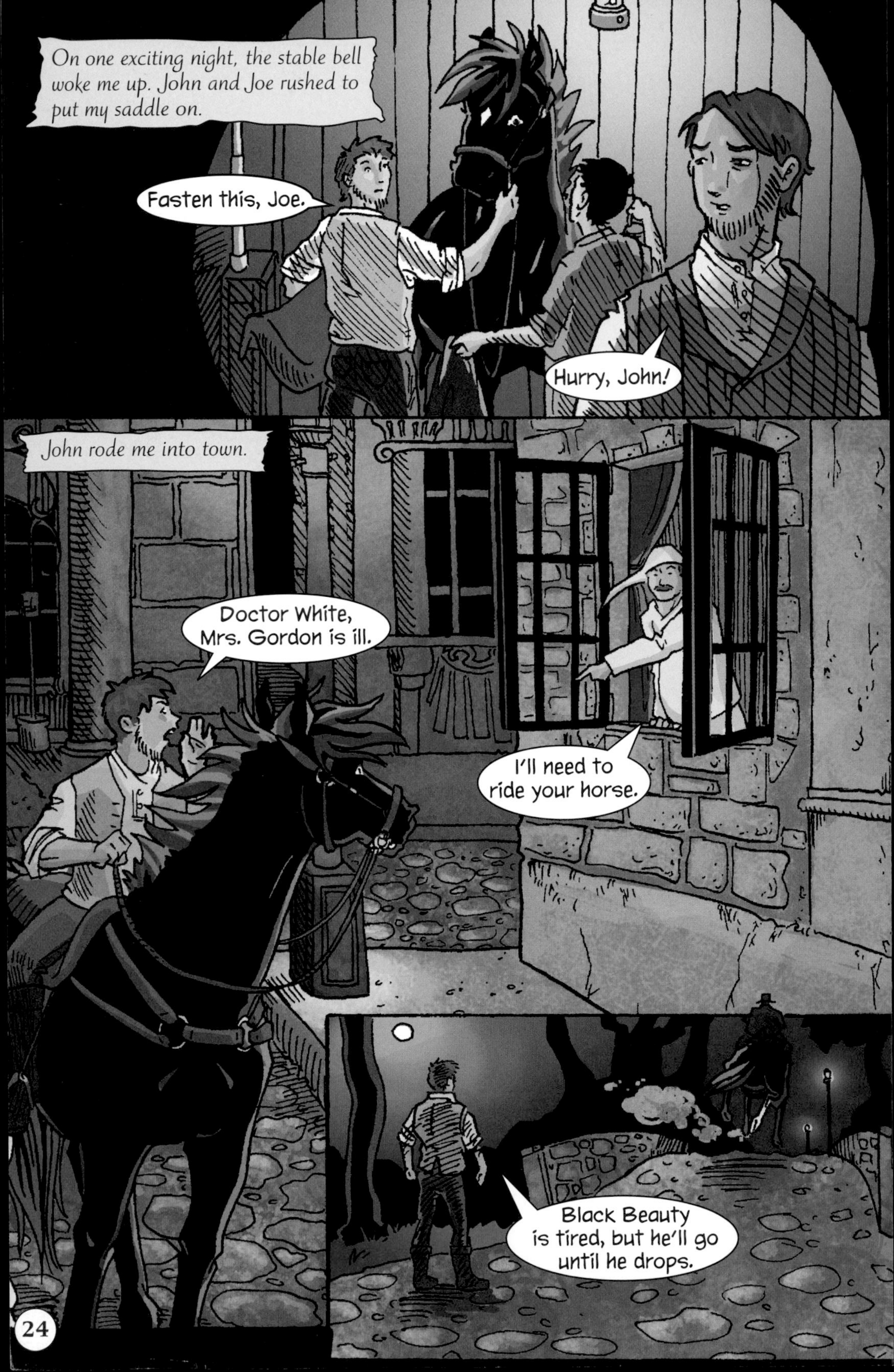
On one exciting night, the stable bell woke me up. John and Joe rushed to put my saddle on.
Fasten this, Joe.
Hurry, John!
John rode me into town.
Doctor White, Mrs. Gordon is ill.
I'll need to ride your horse.
Black Beauty is tired, but he'll go until he drops.

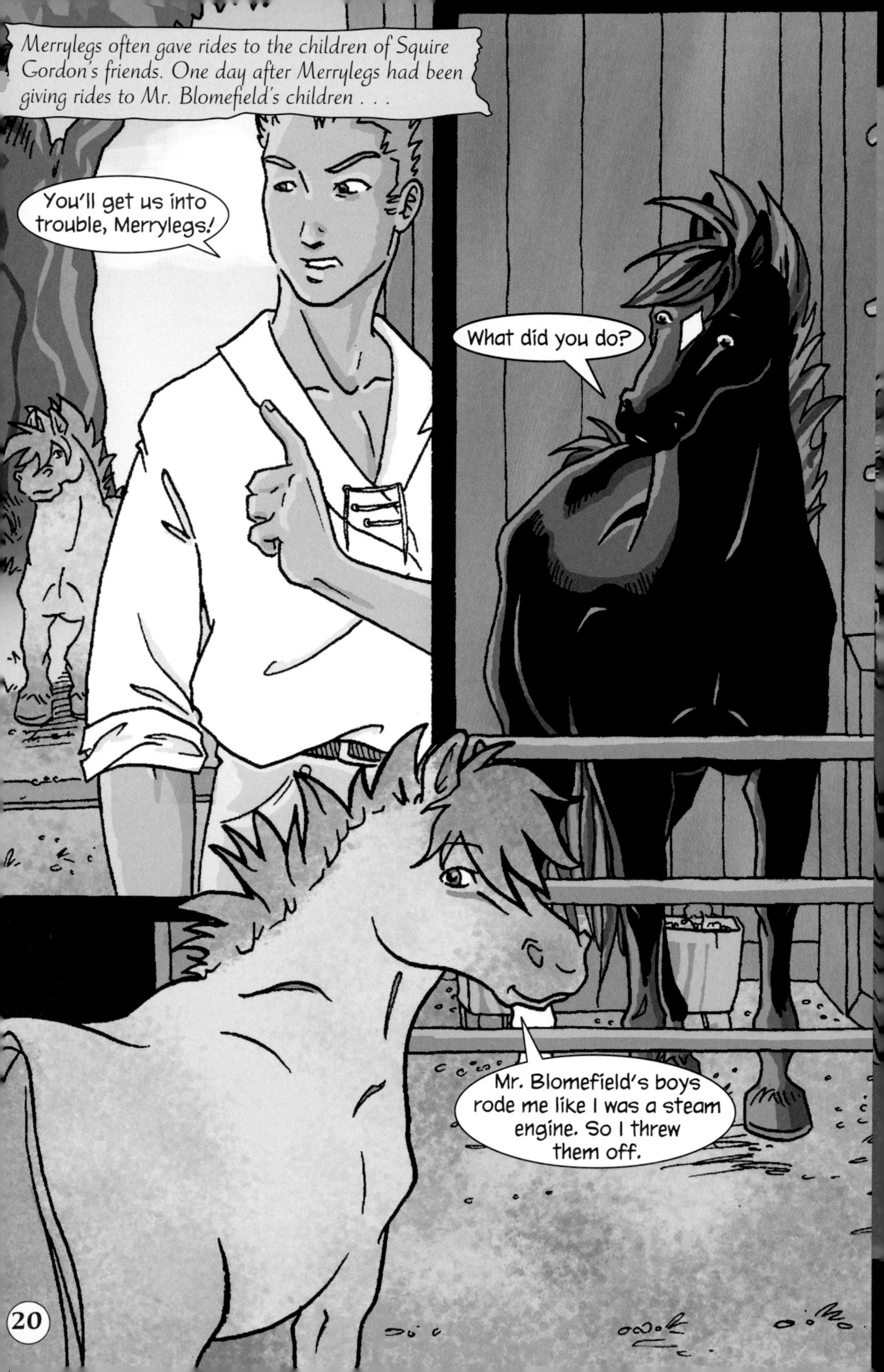
Merrylegs often gave rides to the children of Squire Gordon's friends. One day after Merrylegs had been giving rides to Mr. Blomefield's children . . .
You'll get us into trouble, Merrylegs!
What did you do?
Mr. Blomefield's boys rode me like I was a steam engine. So I threw them off.

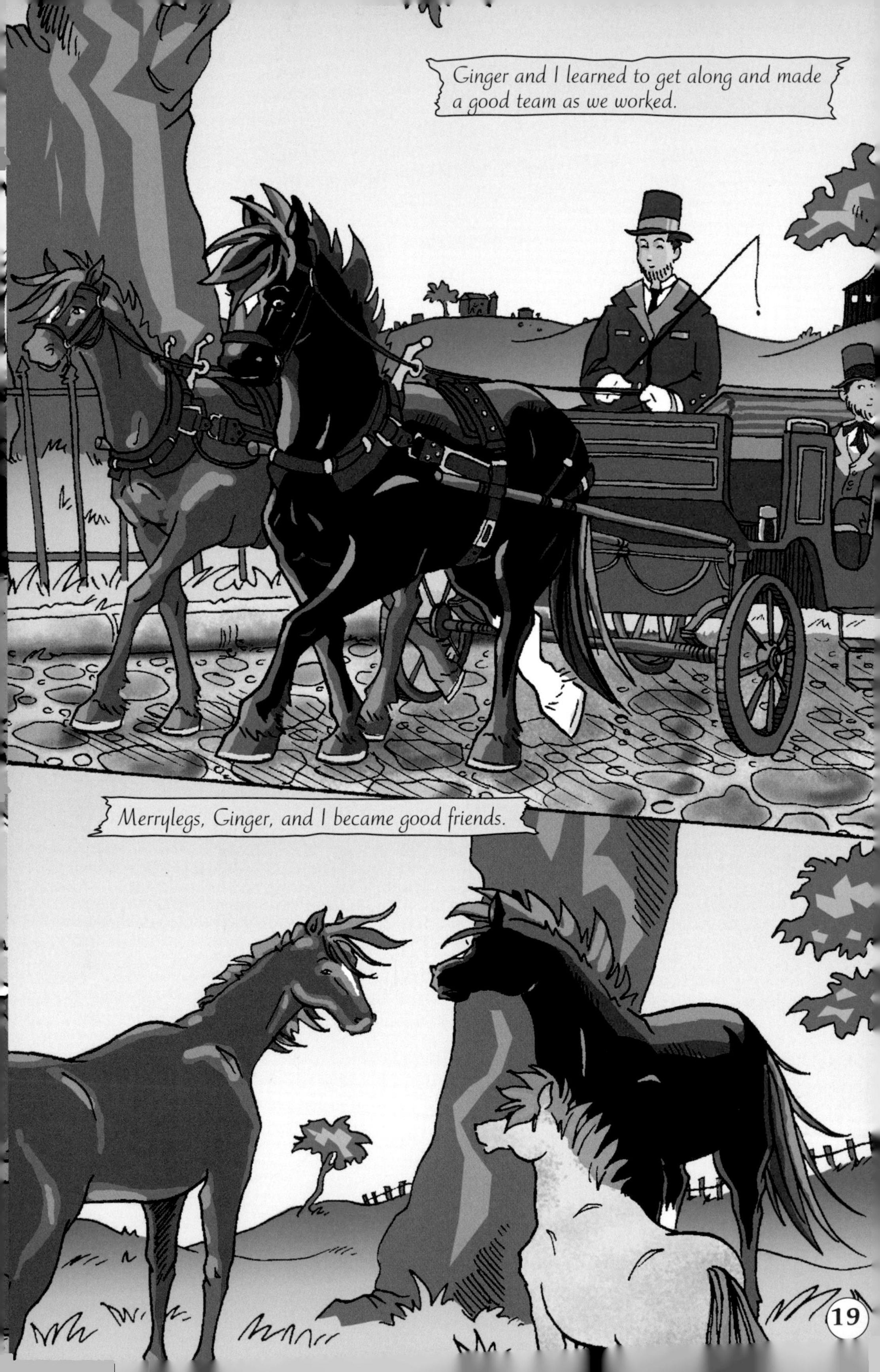
Ginger and I learned to get along and made a good team as we worked.
Merrylegs, Ginger, and I became good friends.

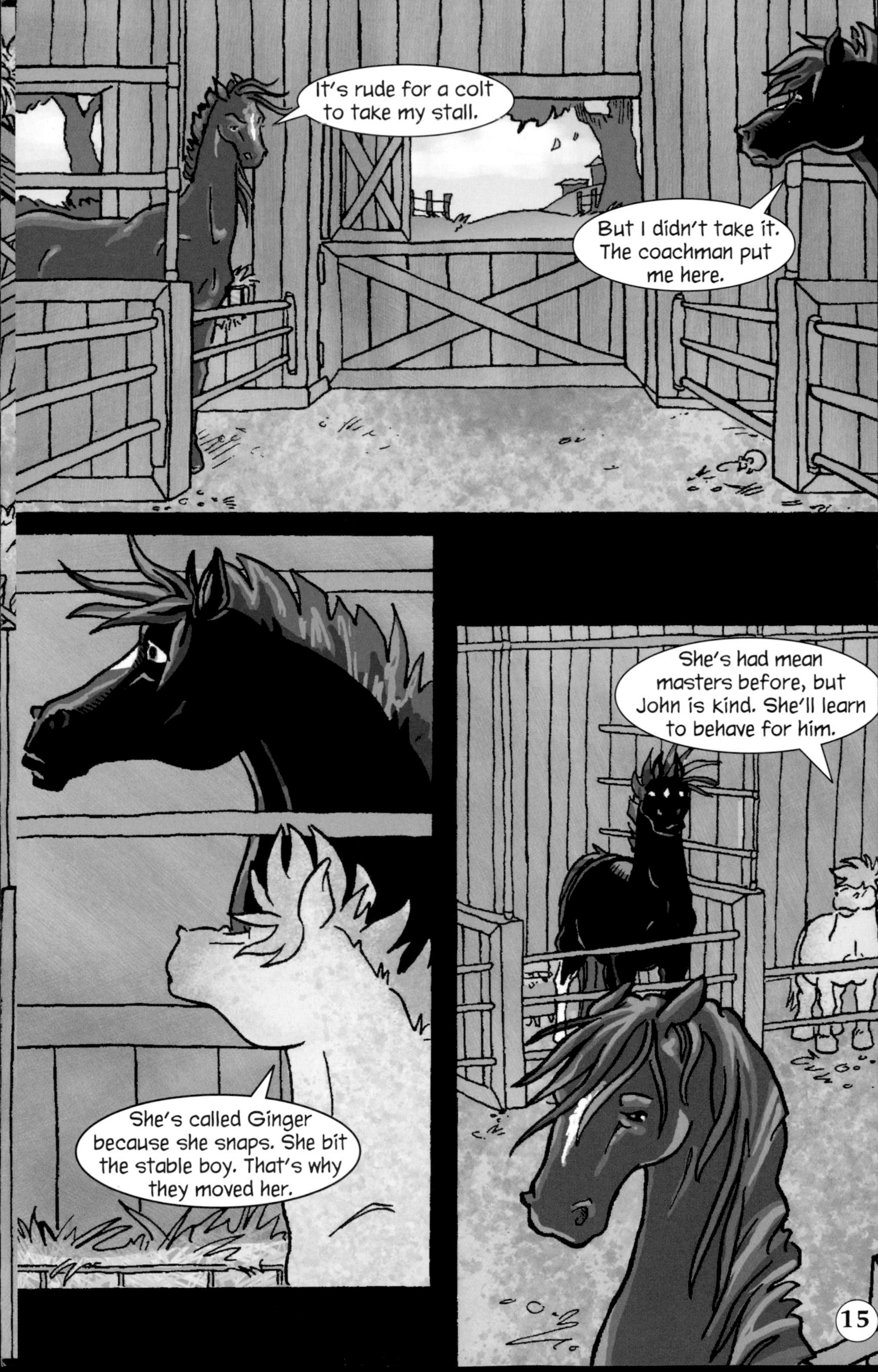
It's rude for a colt to take my stall.
But I didn't take it. The coachman put me here.
She's called Ginger because she snaps. She bit the stable boy. That's why they moved her.
She's had mean masters before, but John is kind. She'll learn to behave for him.

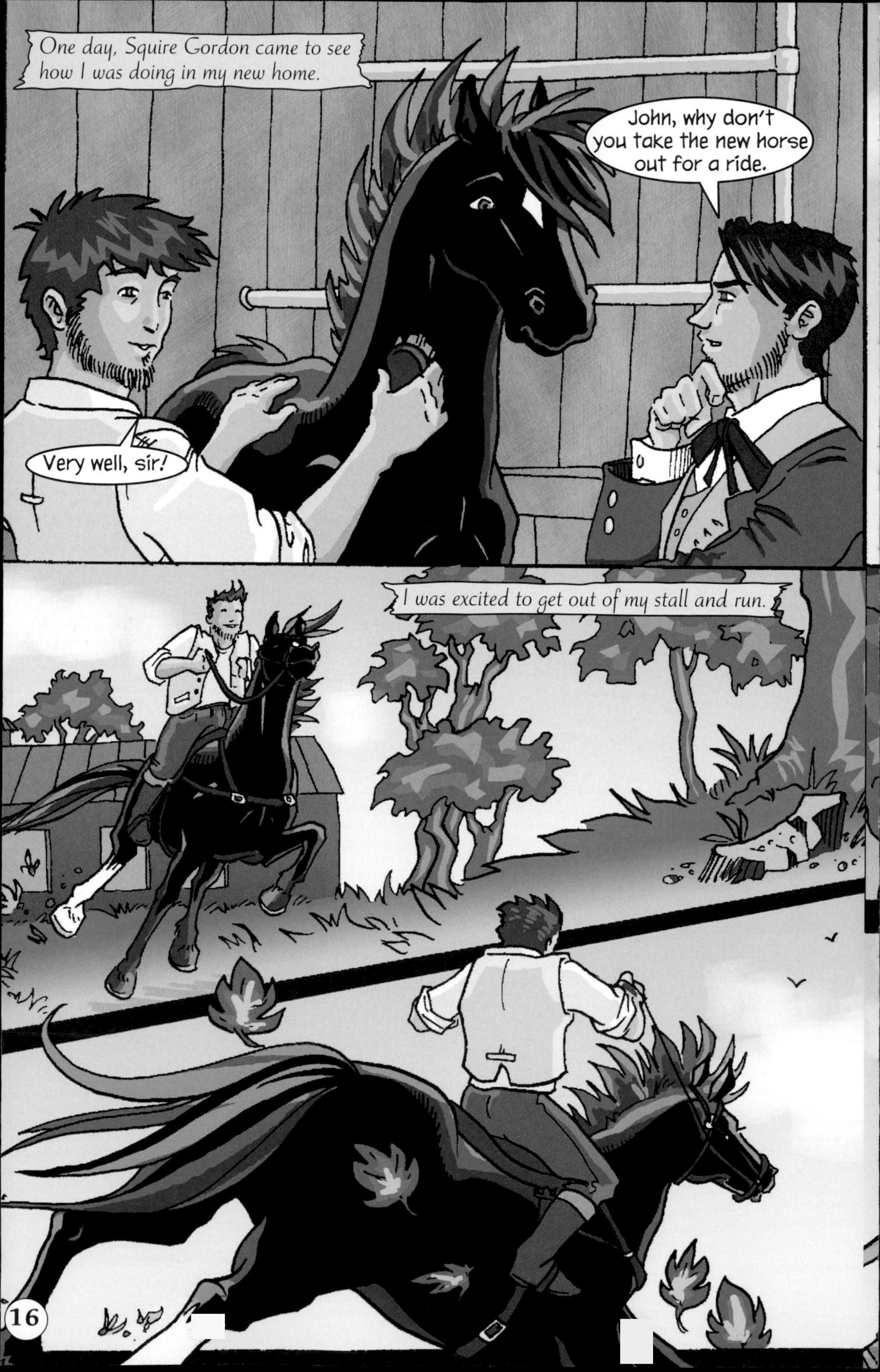
One day, Squire Gordon came to see how I was doing in my new home.
John, why don't you take the new horse out for a ride.
Very well, sir!
I was excited to get out of my stall and run.

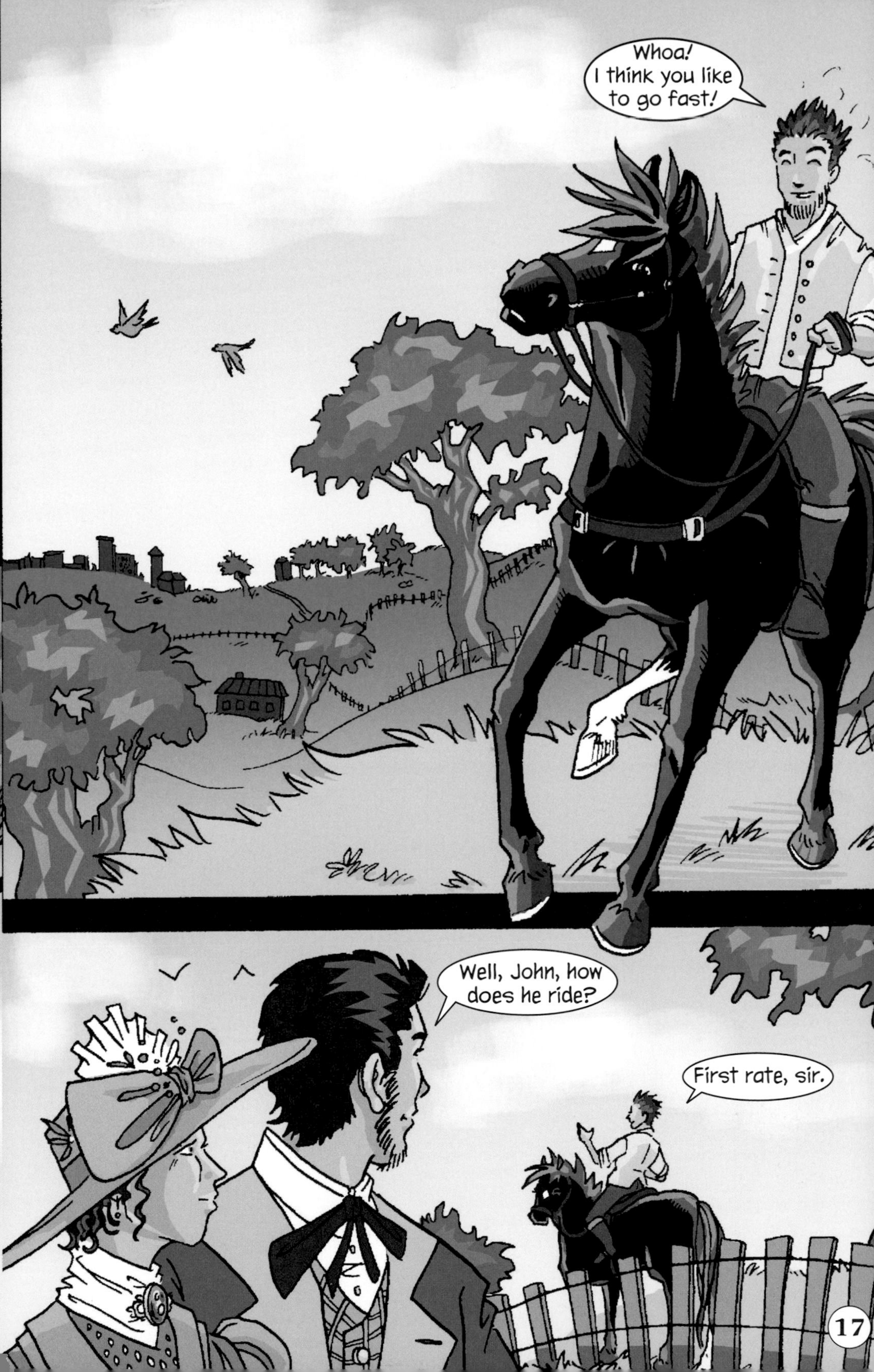
Whoa! I think you like to go fast!
Well, John, how does he ride?
First rate, sir.

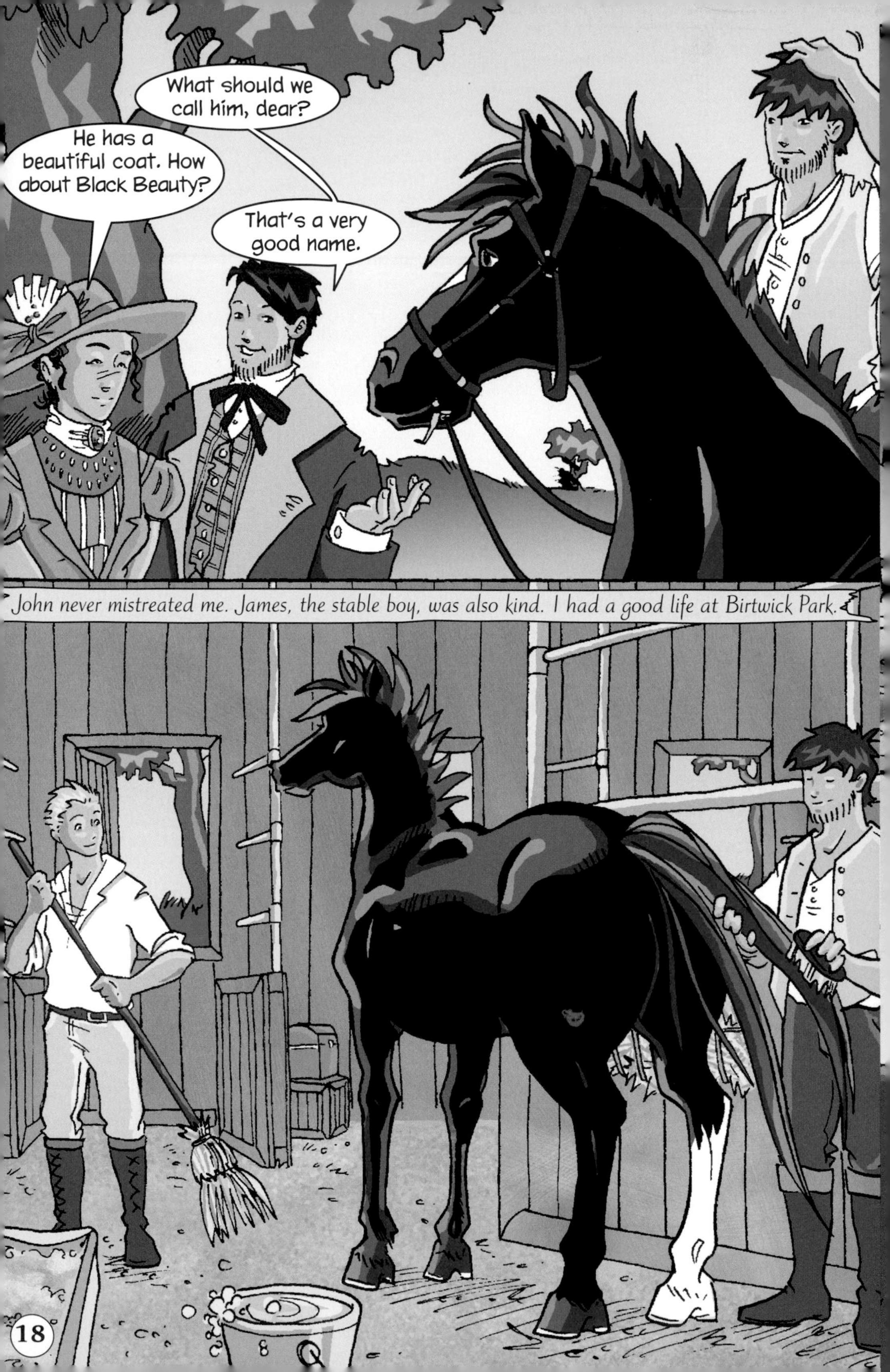
What should we call him, dear?
He has a beautiful coat. How about Black Beauty?
That's a very good name.
John never mistreated me. James, the stable boy, was also kind. I had a good life at Birtwick Park.

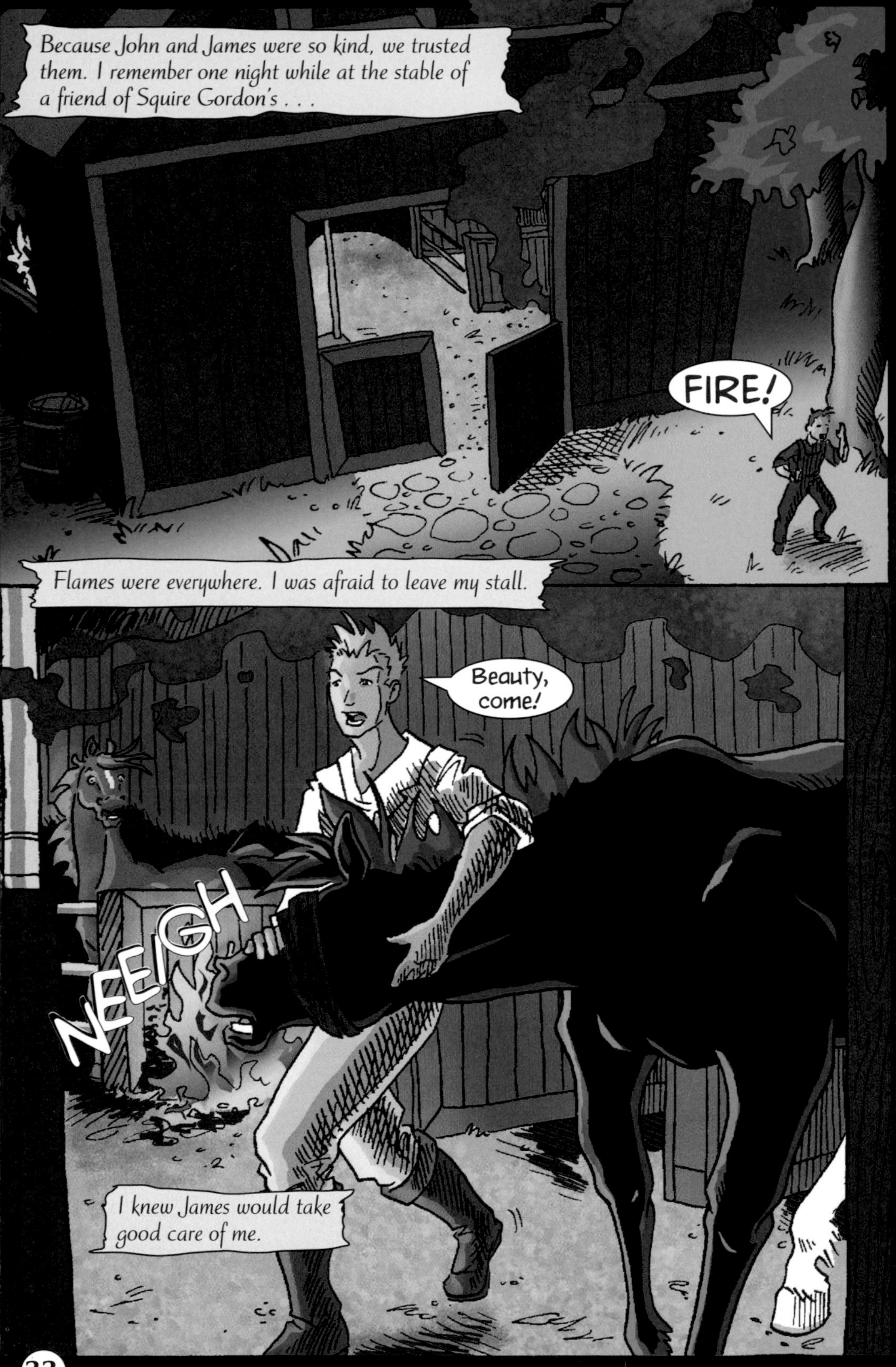
Because John and James were so kind, we trusted them. I remember one night while at the stable of a friend of Squire Gordon's . . .
FIRE!
Flames were everywhere. I was afraid to leave my stall.
Beauty, come!
NEEIGH
I knew James would take good care of me.

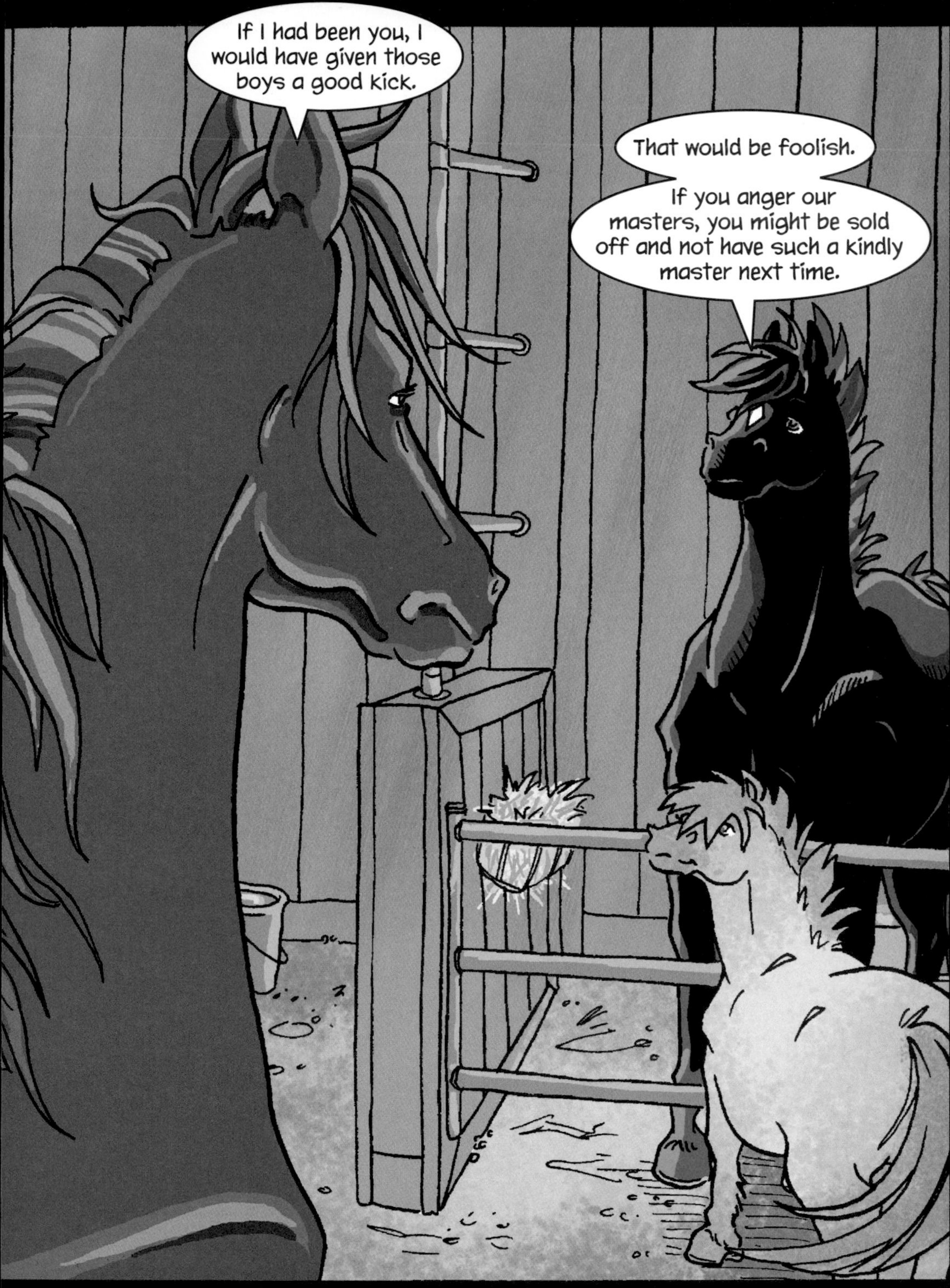
If I had been you, I would have given those boys a good kick.
That would be foolish.
If you anger our masters, you might be sold off and not have such a kindly master next time.

Black Beauty

Joe Green
A stable boy

Merrylegs
Black Beauty's stable mate
and friend at Birtwick Park.

Chapter 1 ★ My Early Home

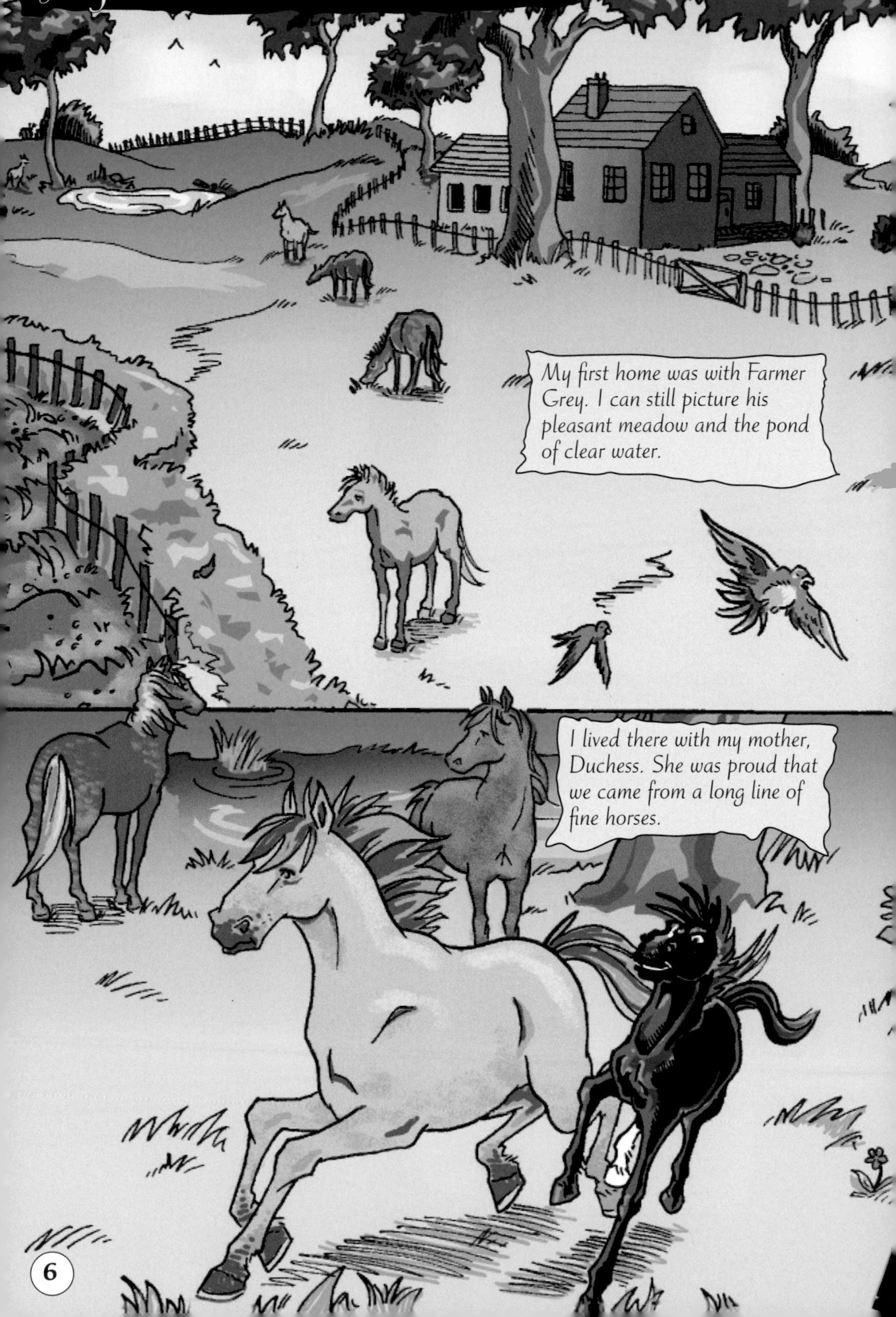
My first home was with Farmer Grey. I can still picture his pleasant meadow and the pond of clear water.
I lived there with my mother, Duchess. She was proud that we came from a long line of fine horses.

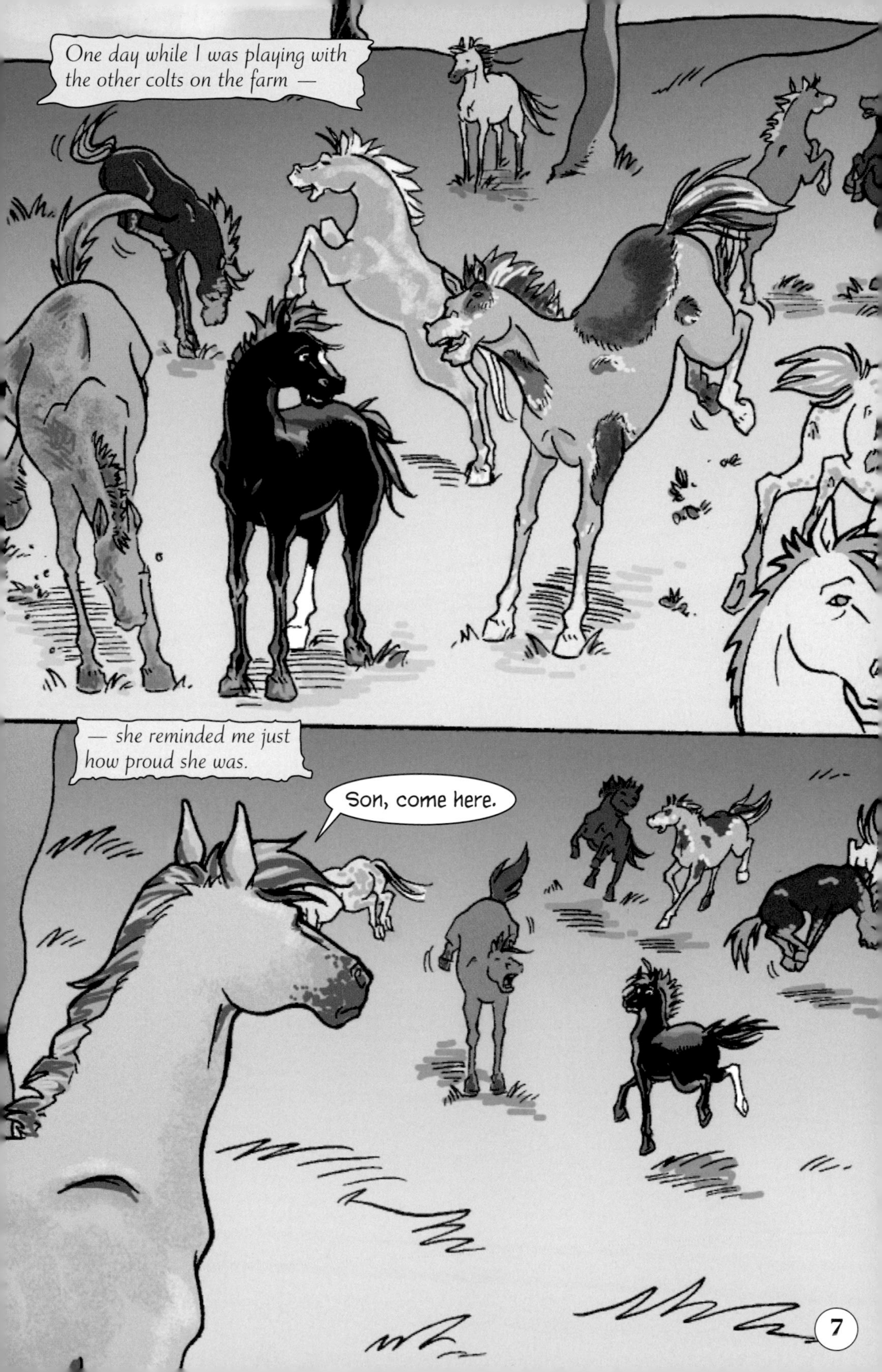
One day while I was playing with the other colts on the farm —
— she reminded me just how proud she was.
Son, come here.

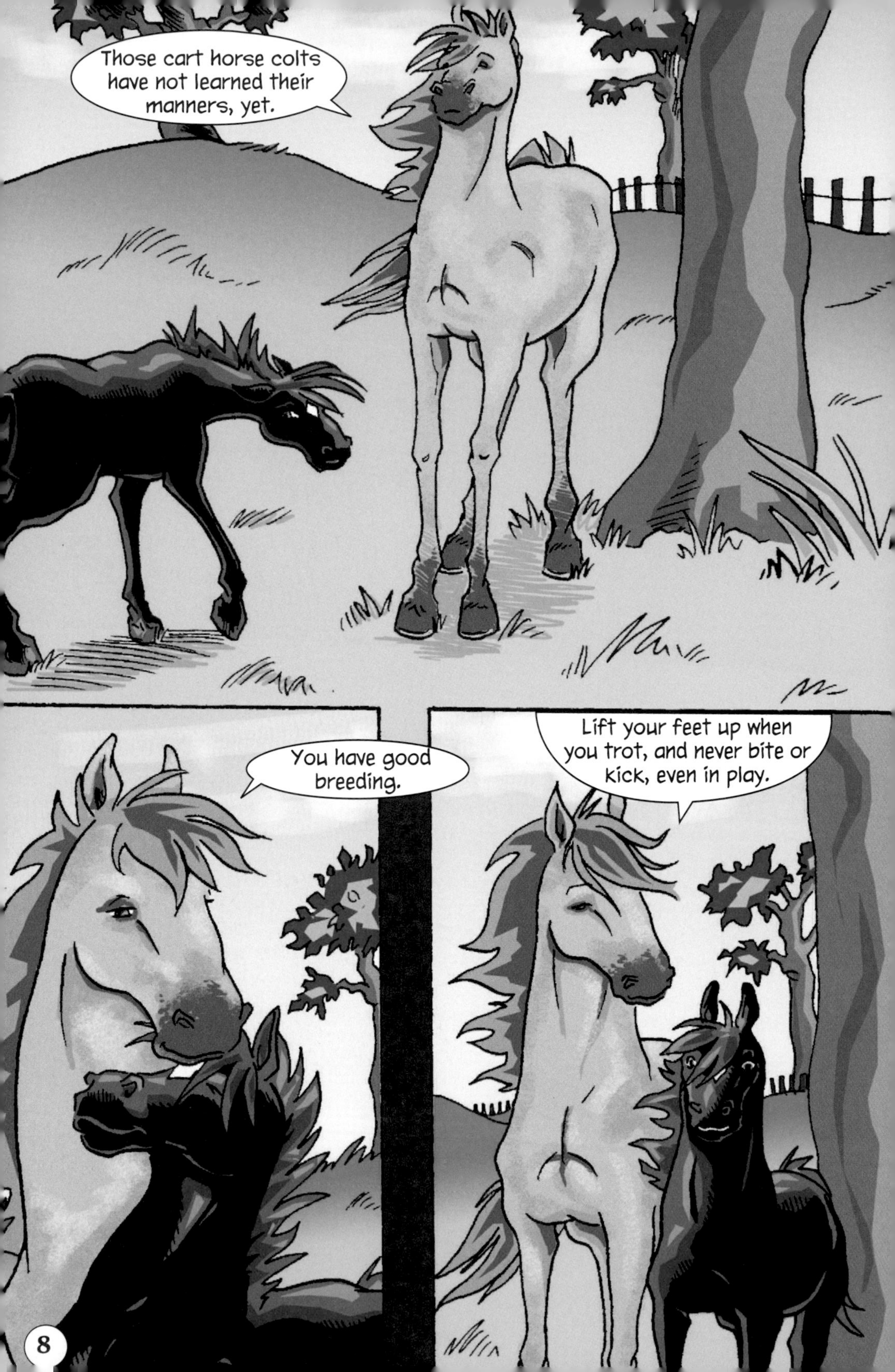
Those cart horse colts have not learned their manners, yet.
You have good breeding.
Lift your feet up when you trot, and never bite or kick, even in play.

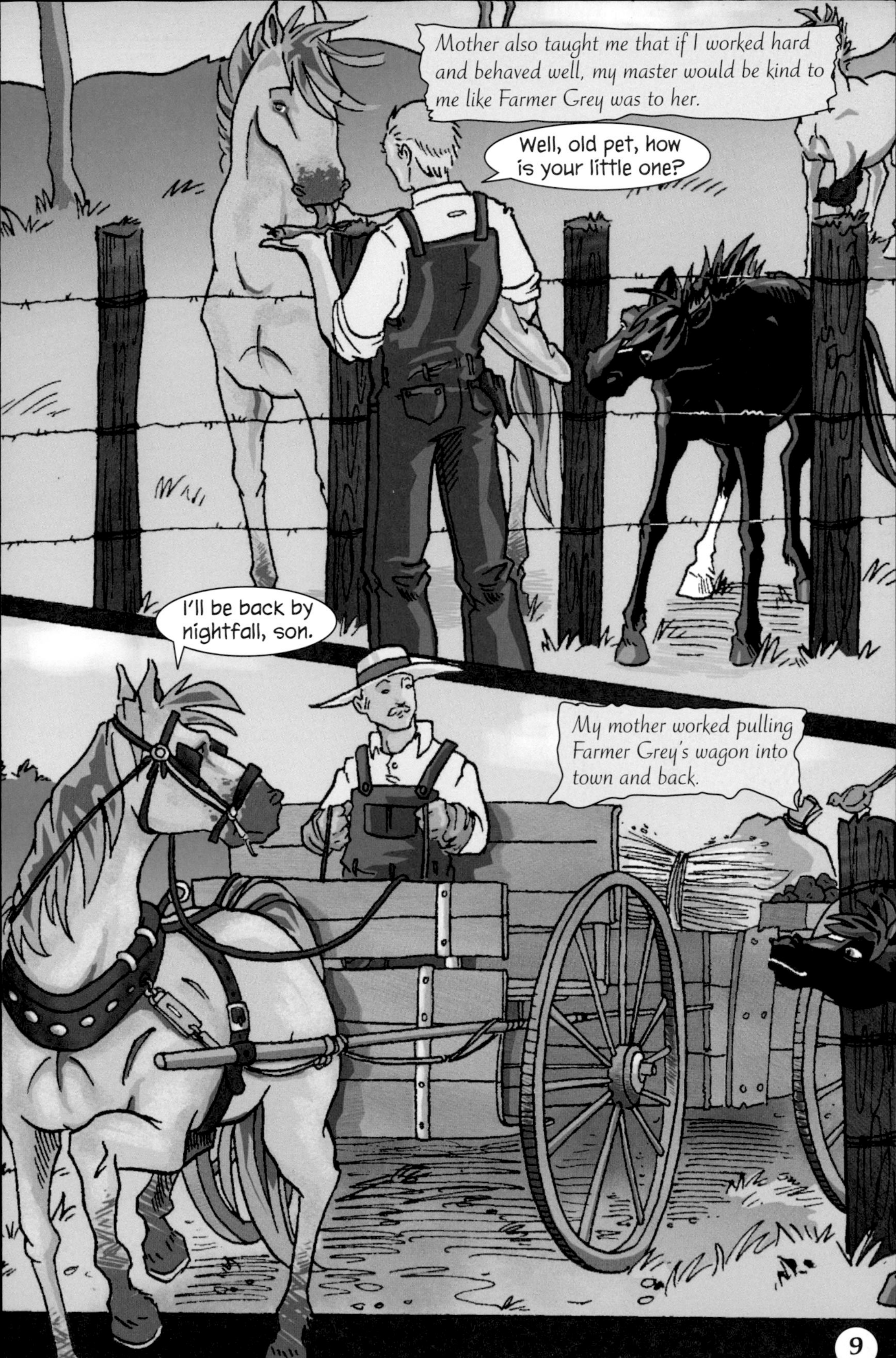
Mother also taught me that if I worked hard and behaved well, my master would be kind to me like Farmer Grey was to her.
Well, old pet, how is your little one?
I'll be back by nightfall, son.
My mother worked pulling Farmer Grey's wagon into town and back.

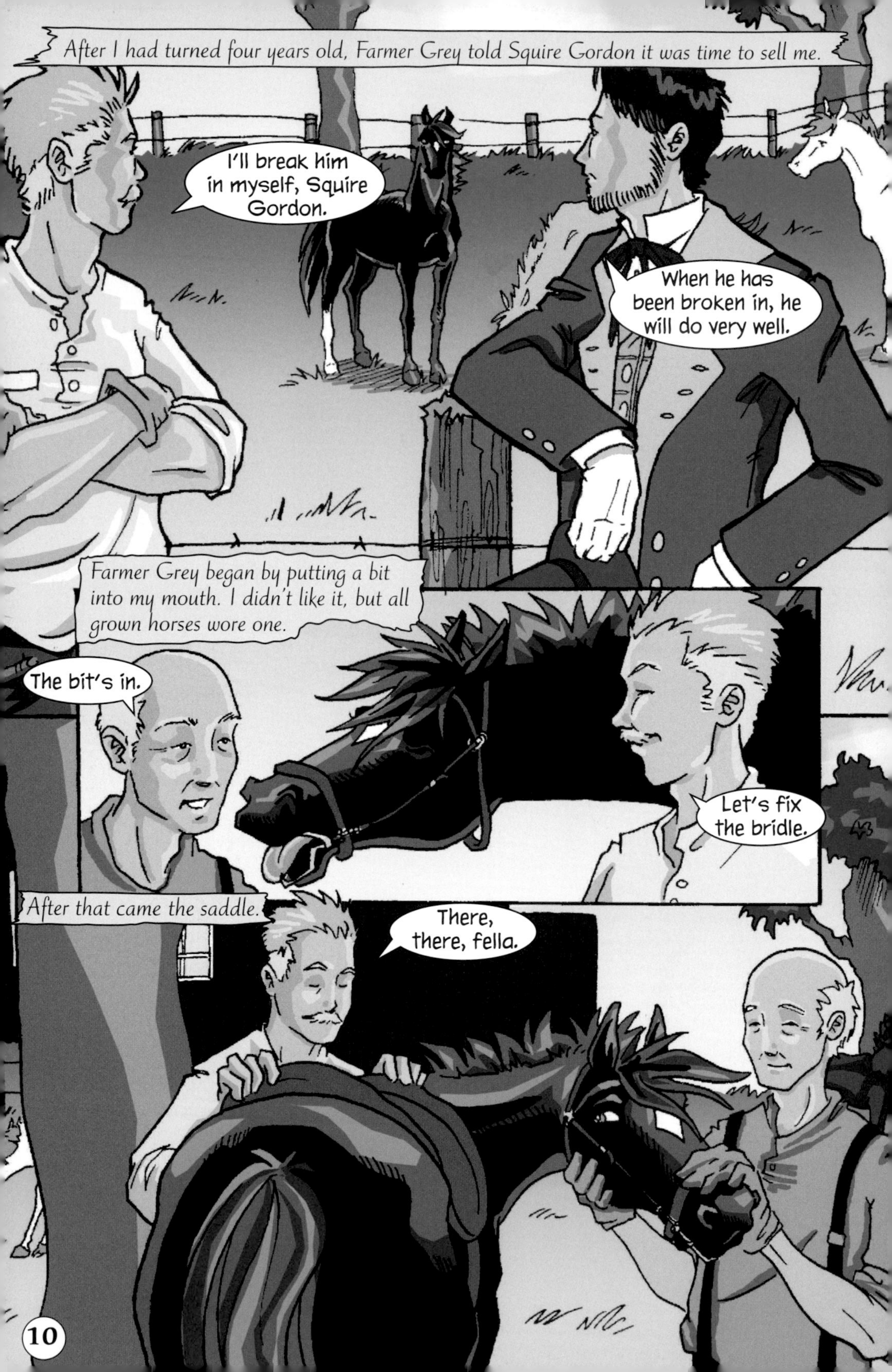
After I had turned four years old, Farmer Grey told Squire Gordon it was time to sell me.
I'll break him in myself, Squire Gordon.
When he has been broken in, he will do very well.
Farmer Grey began by putting a bit into my mouth. I didn't like it, but all grown horses wore one.
The bit's in.
Let's fix the bridle.
After that came the saddle.
There, there, fella.

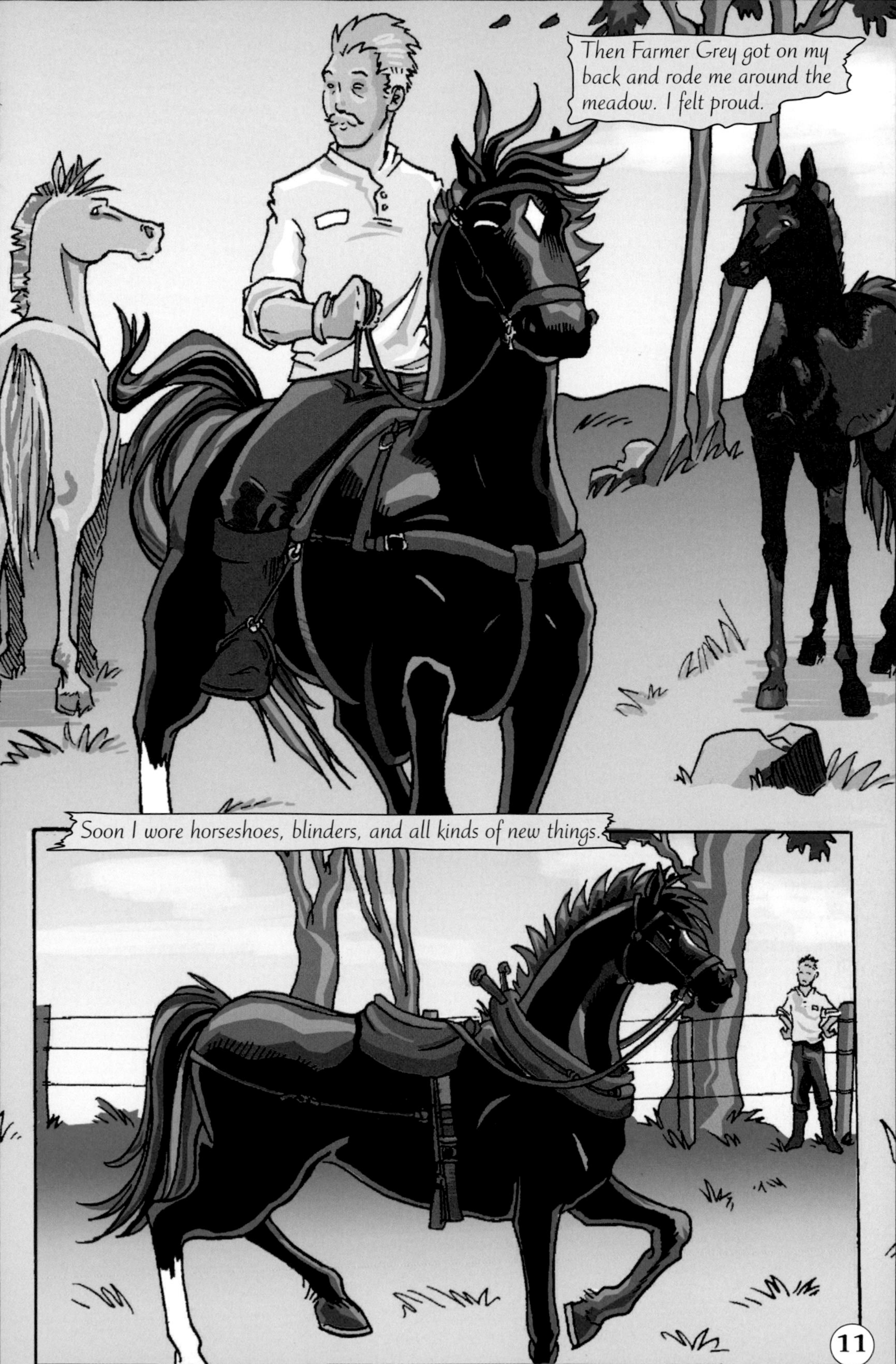
Then Farmer Grey got on my back and rode me around the meadow. I felt proud.
Soon I wore horseshoes, blinders, and all kinds of new things.

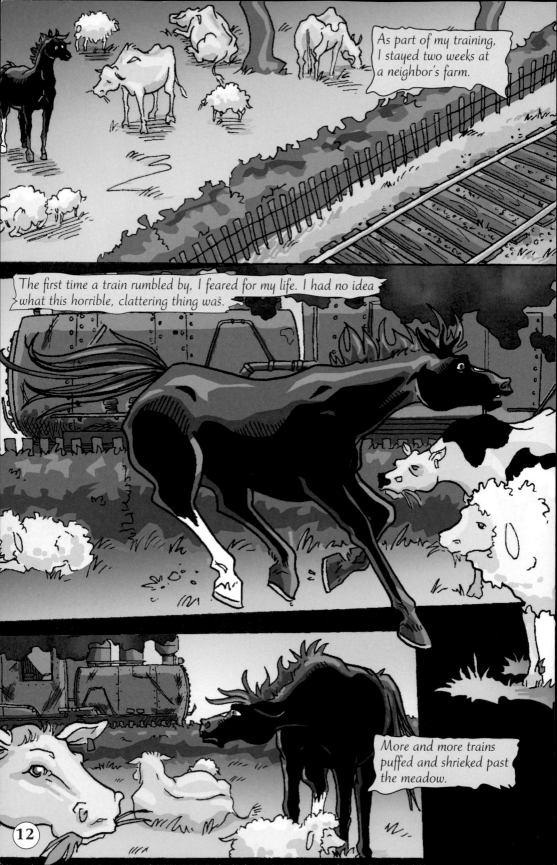

As part of my training, I stayed two weeks at a neighbor's farm.

The first time a train rumbled by, I feared for my life. I had no idea what this horrible, clattering thing was.

More and more trains puffed and shrieked past the meadow.

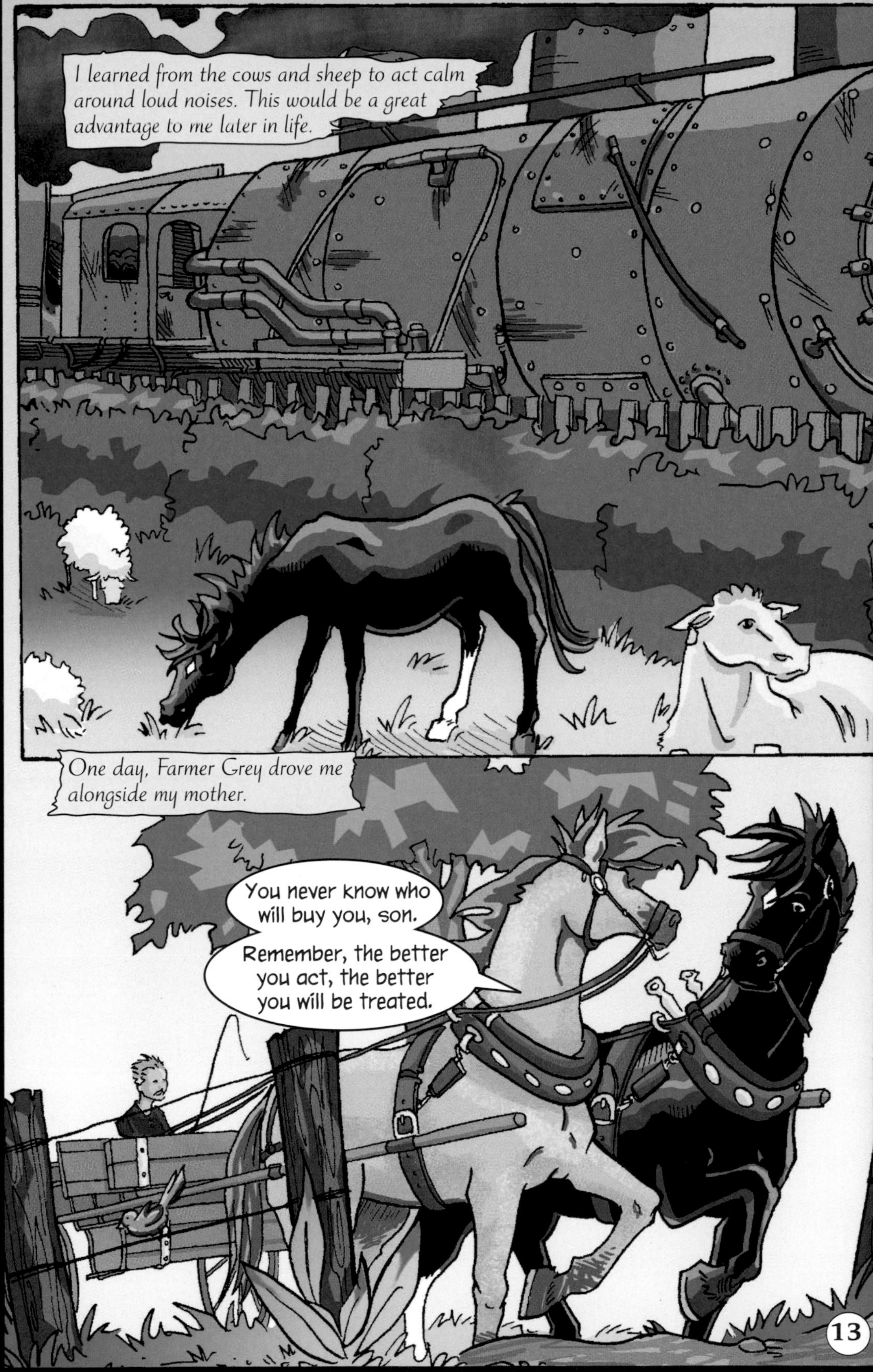

I learned from the cows and sheep to act calm around loud noises. This would be a great advantage to me later in life.
One day, Farmer Grey drove me alongside my mother.
You never know who will buy you, son.
Remember, the better you act, the better you will be treated.

Chapter 2 ★ Birtwick Park

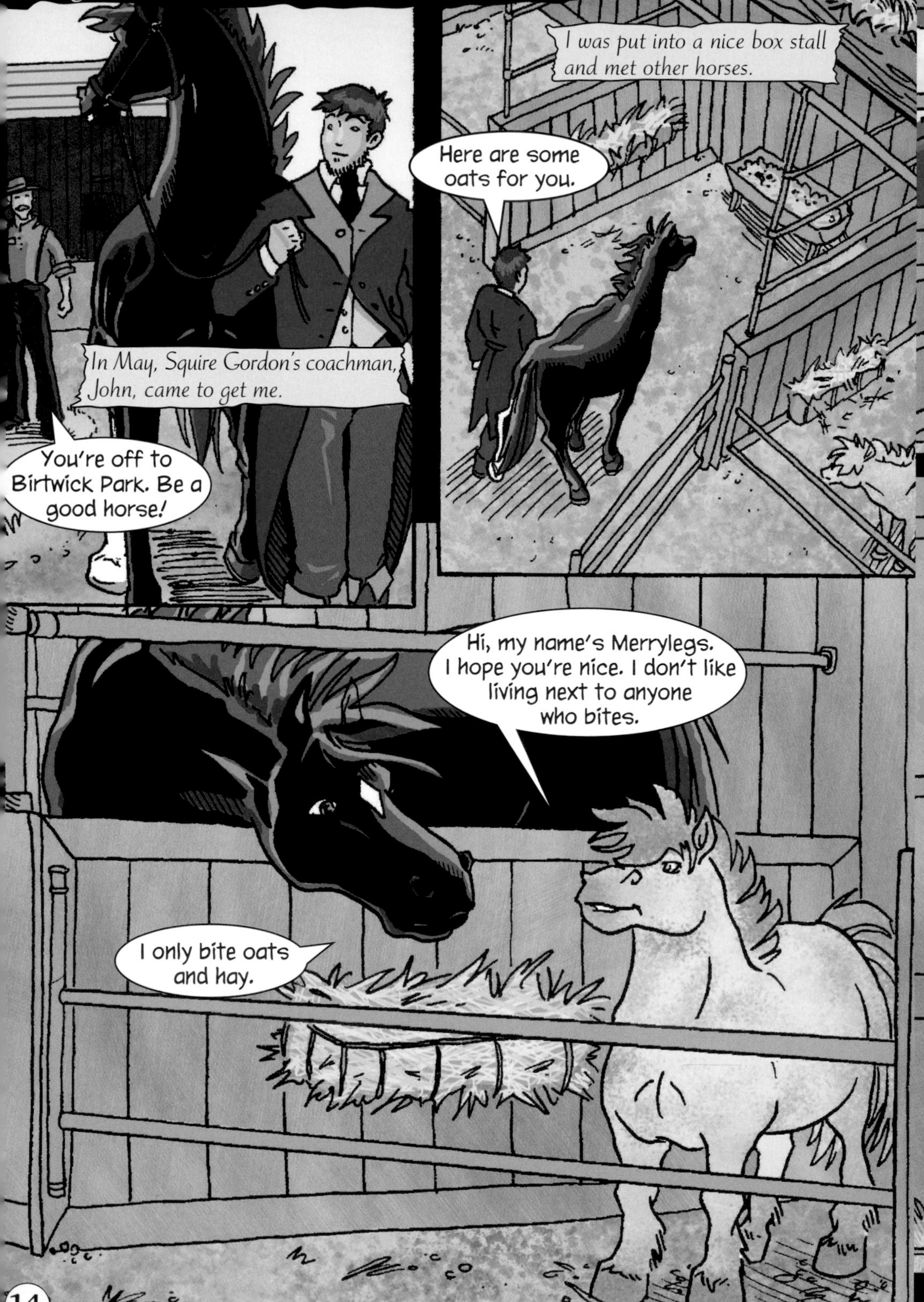
In May, Squire Gordon's coachman, John, came to get me.
You're off to Birtwick Park. Be a good horse!
I was put into a nice box stall and met other horses.
Here are some oats for you.
Hi, my name's Merrylegs. I hope you're nice. I don't like living next to anyone who bites.
I only bite oats and hay.

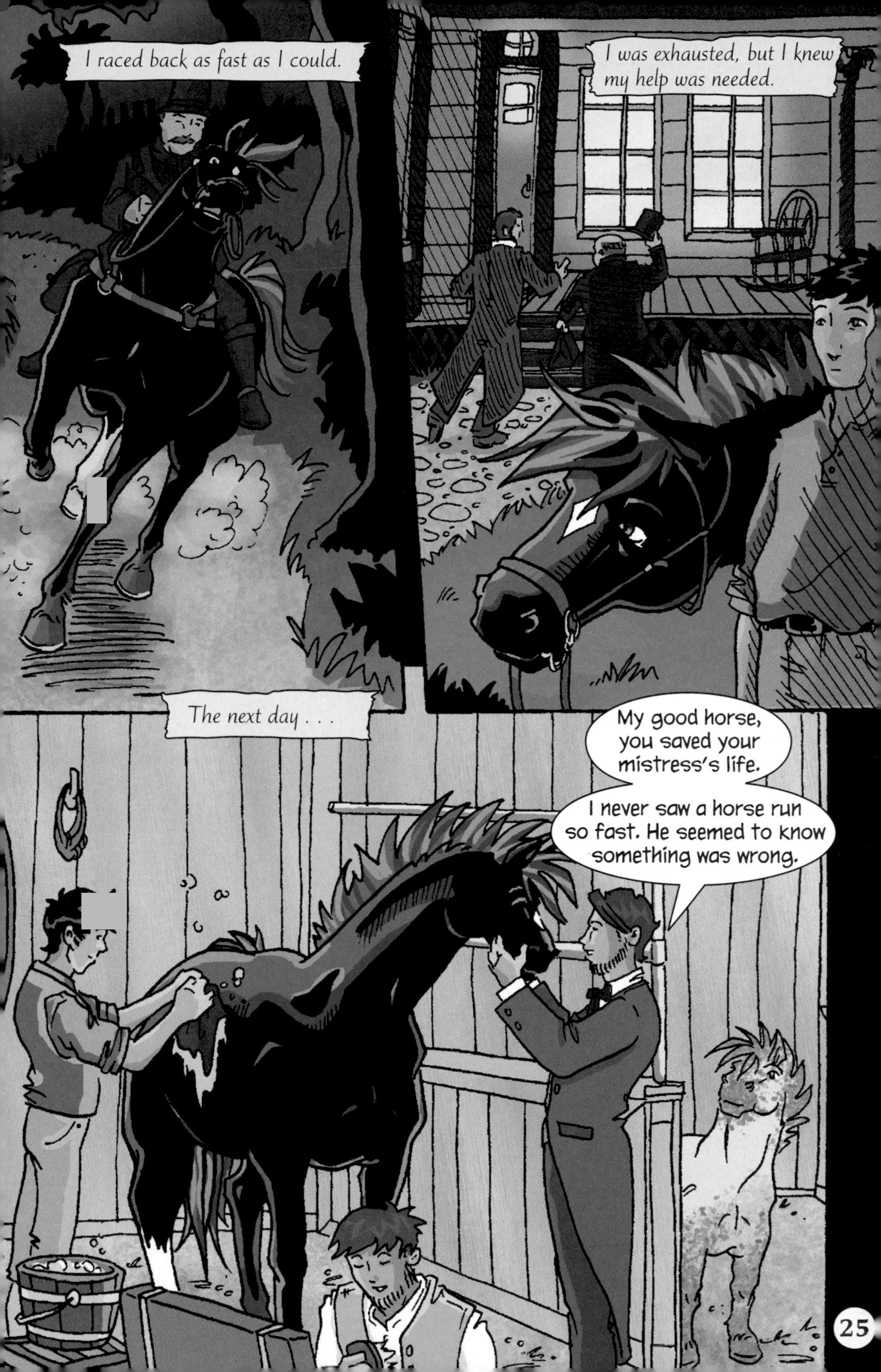
I raced back as fast as I could.
I was exhausted, but I knew my help was needed.
The next day . . .
My good horse, you saved your mistress's life.
I never saw a horse run so fast. He seemed to know something was wrong.

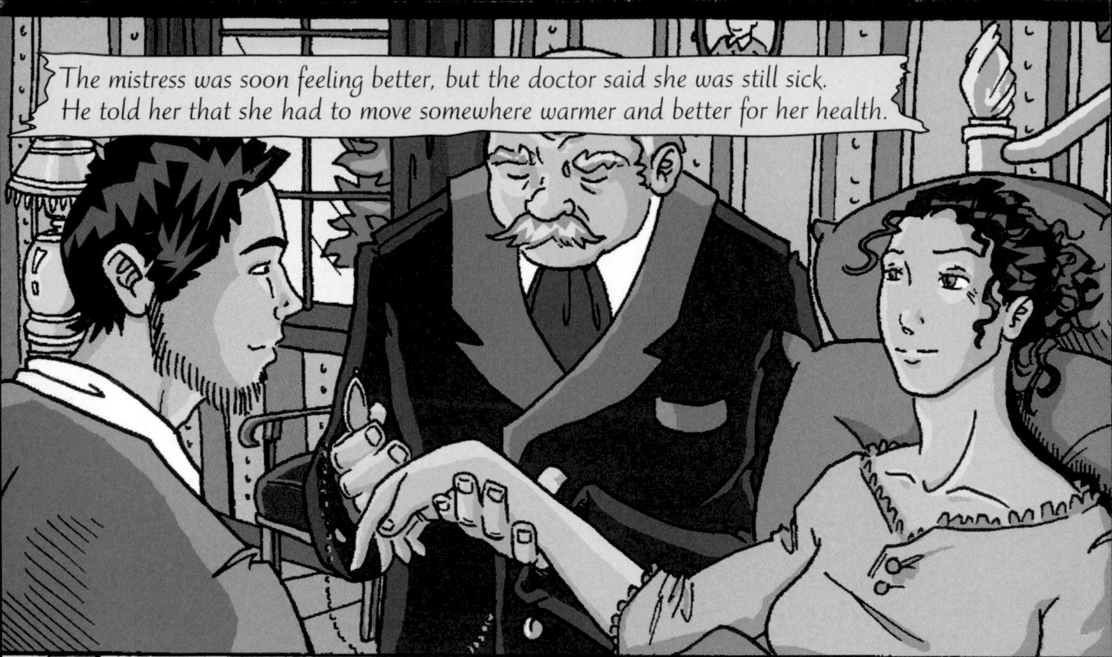
The mistress was soon feeling better, but the doctor said she was still sick. He told her that she had to move somewhere warmer and better for her health.

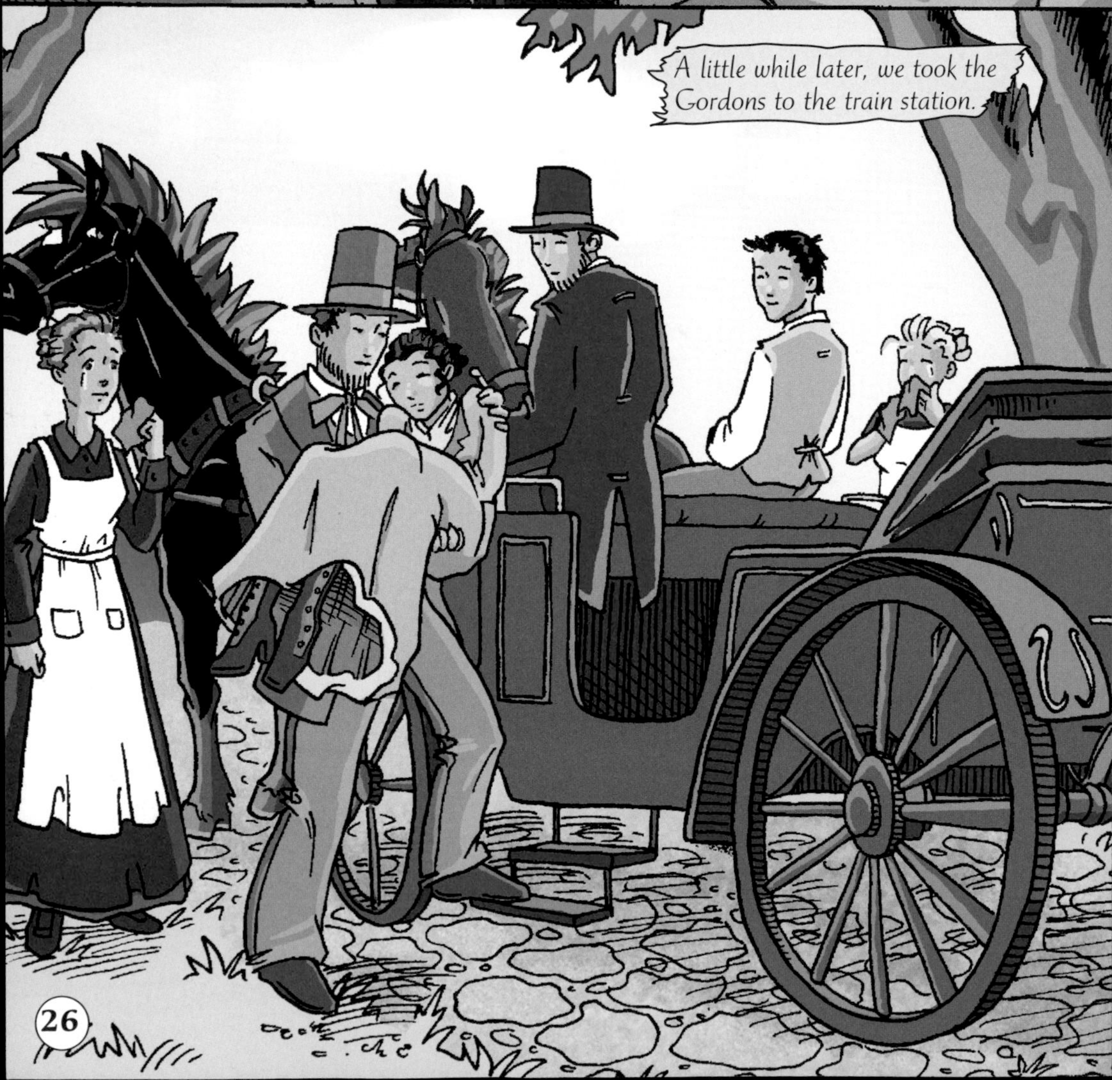
A little while later, we took the Gordons to the train station.

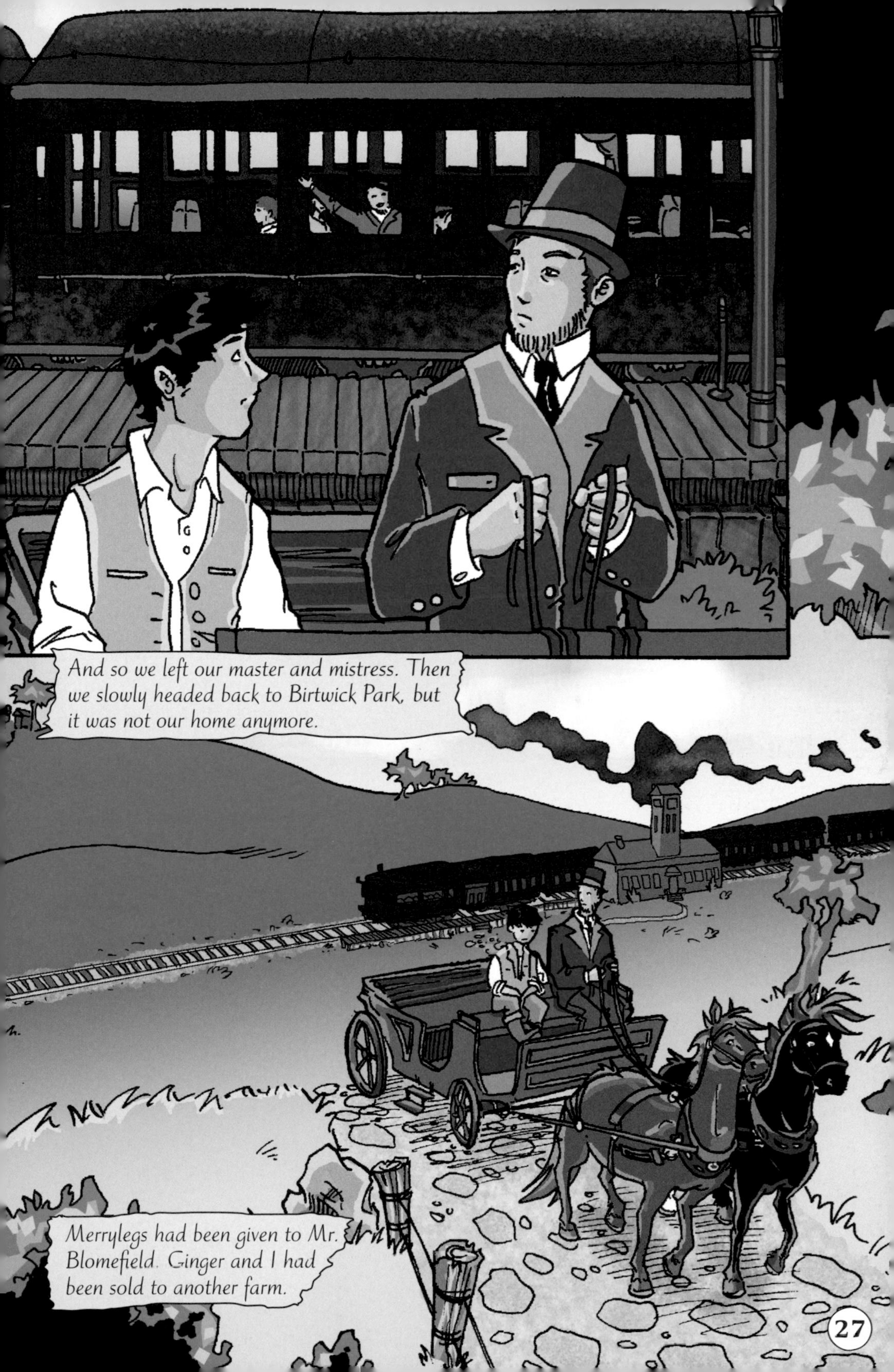
And so we left our master and mistress. Then we slowly headed back to Birtwick Park, but it was not our home anymore.
Merrylegs had been given to Mr. Blomefield. Ginger and I had been sold to another farm.

Chapter 3 ★ Earlshall Park

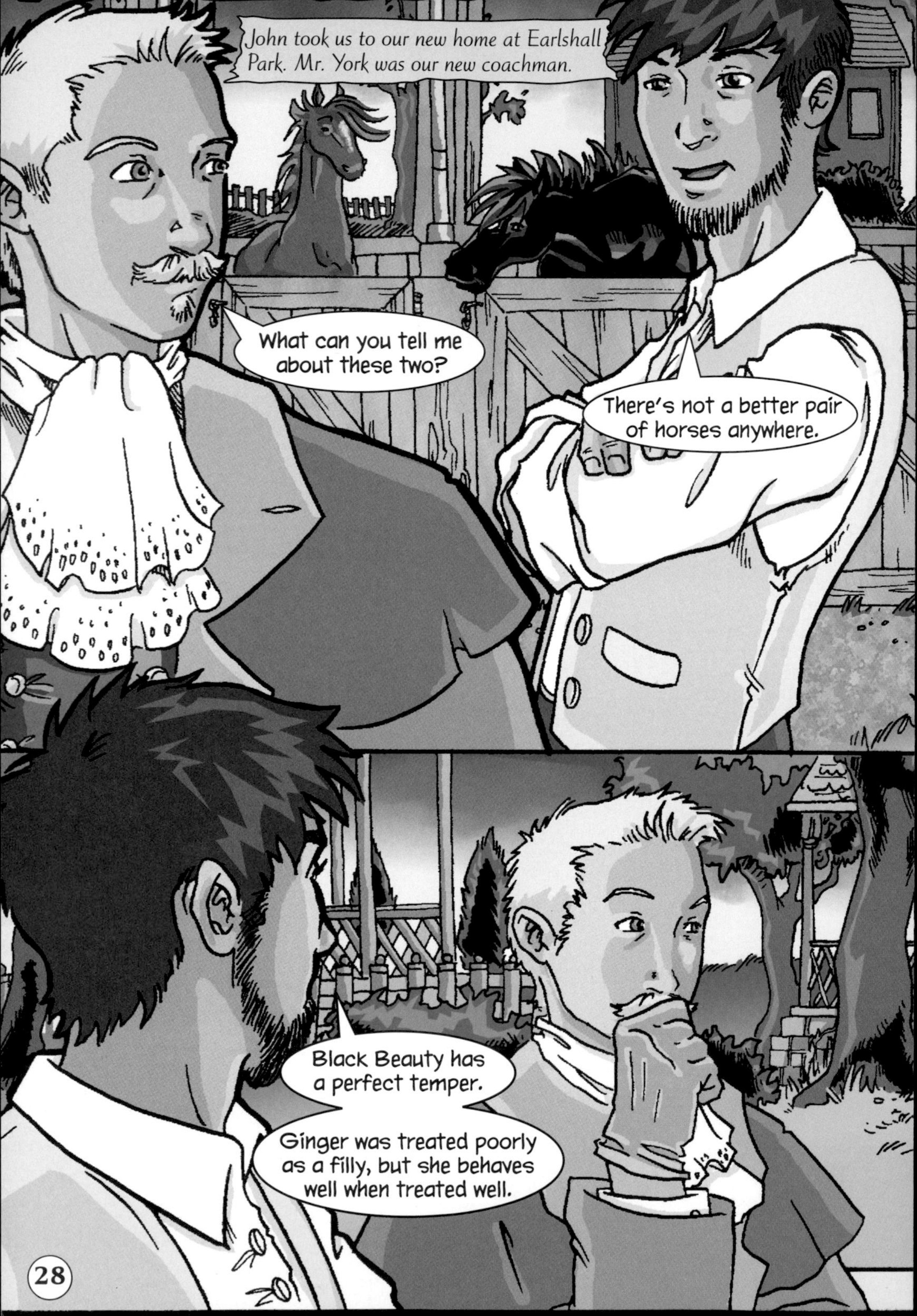
John took us to our new home at Earlshall Park. Mr. York was our new coachman.
What can you tell me about these two?
There's not a better pair of horses anywhere.
Black Beauty has a perfect temper.
Ginger was treated poorly as a filly, but she behaves well when treated well.

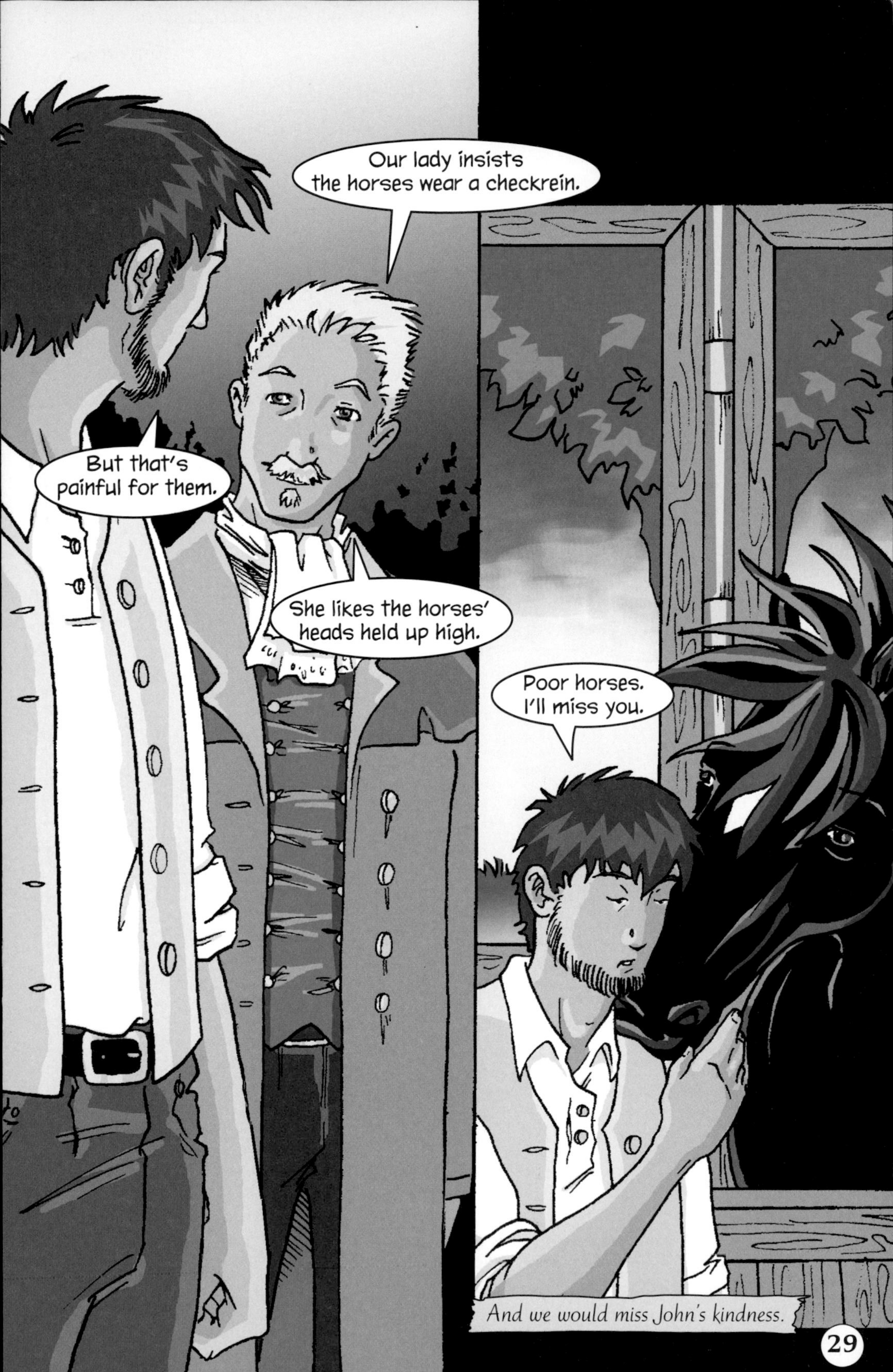

Our lady insists the horses wear a checkrein.
But that's painful for them.
She likes the horses' heads held up high.
Poor horses. I'll miss you.
And we would miss John's kindness.

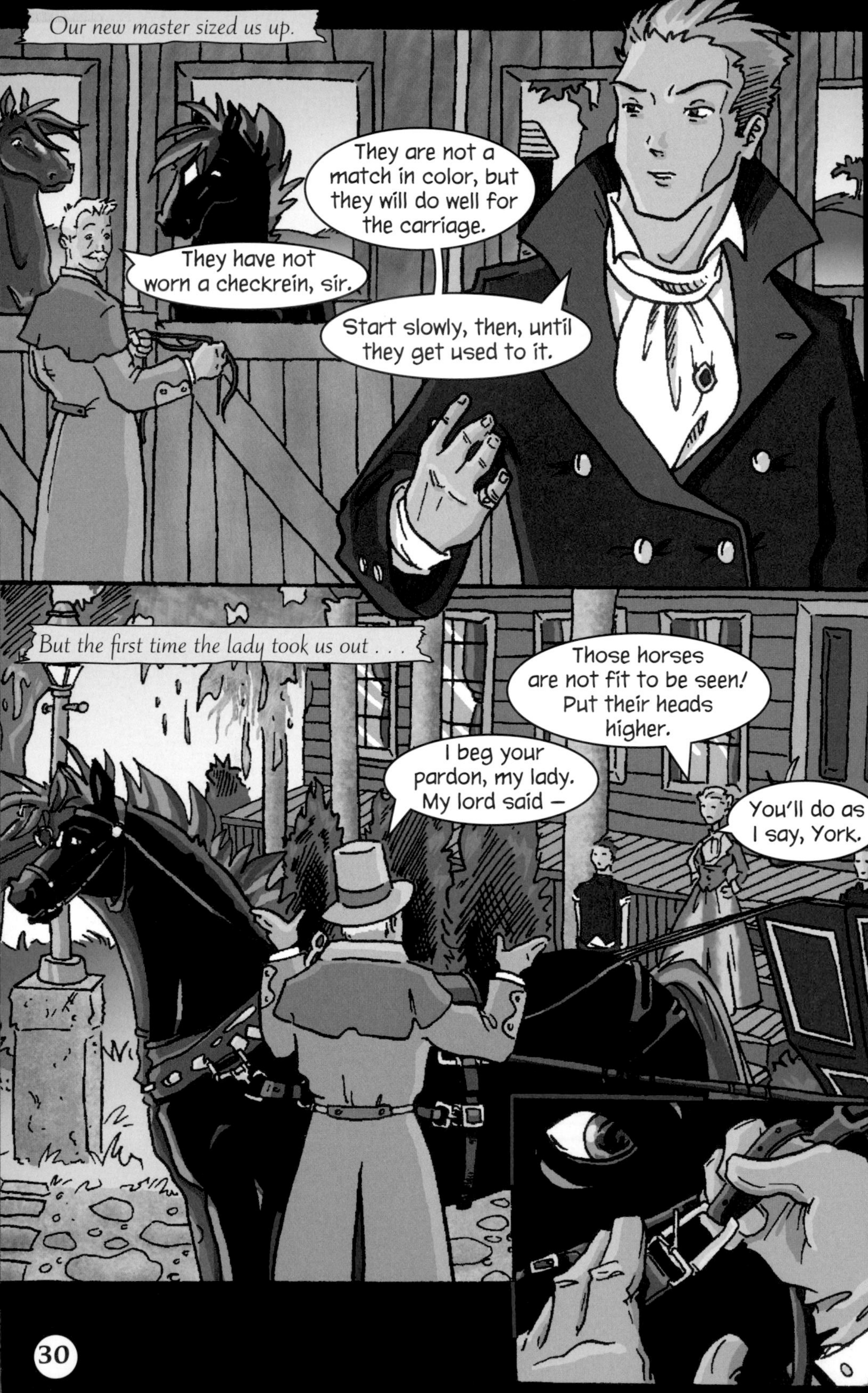
Our new master sized us up.
They are not a match in color, but they will do well for the carriage.
They have not worn a checkrein, sir.
Start slowly, then, until they get used to it.
But the first time the lady took us out . . .
Those horses are not fit to be seen! Put their heads higher.
I beg your pardon, my lady. My lord said –
You'll do as I say, York.

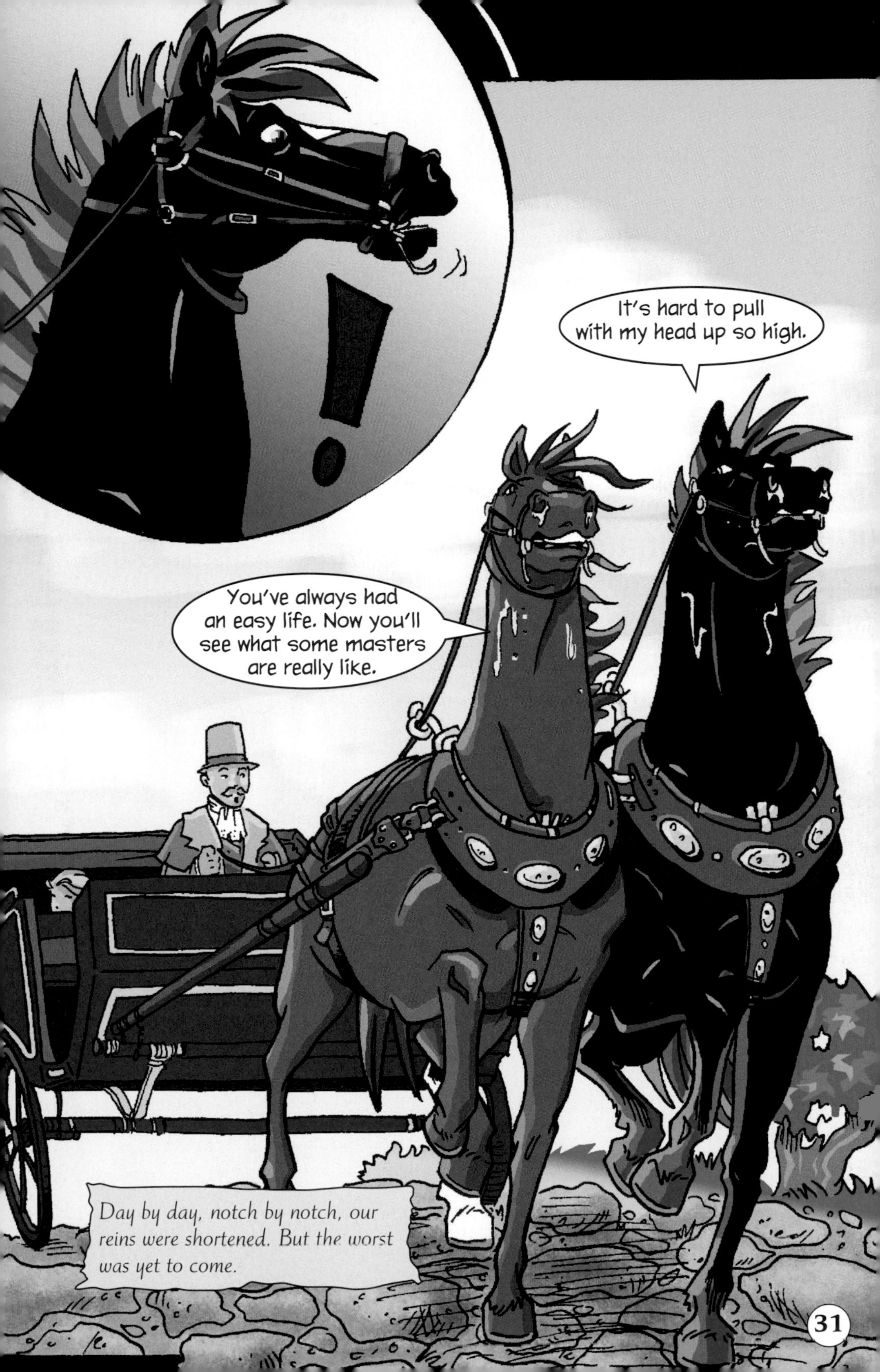
It's hard to pull
with my head up so high.
You've always had
an easy life. Now you'll
see what some masters
are really like.
Day by day, notch by notch, our
reins were shortened. But the worst
was yet to come.

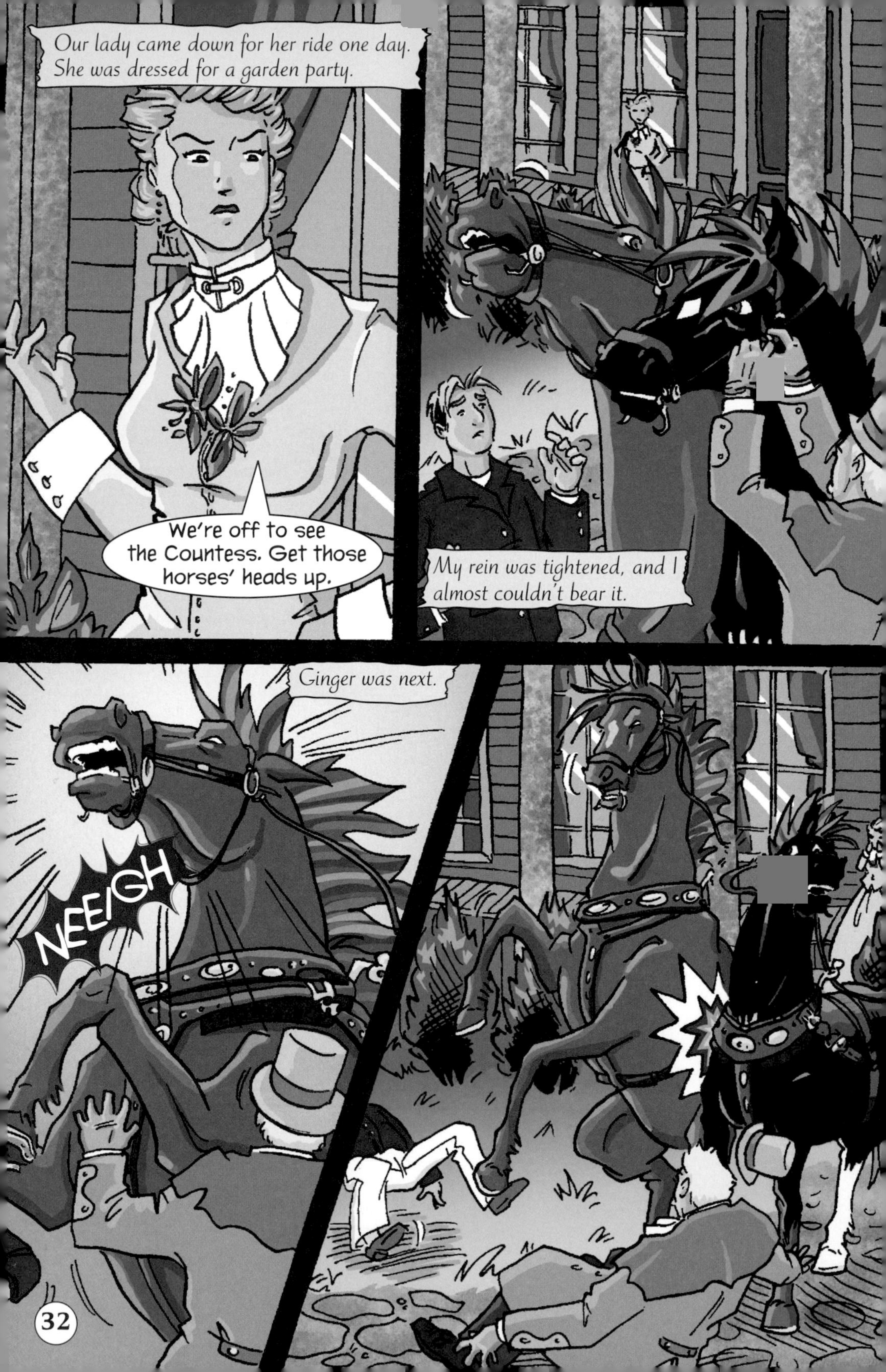
Our lady came down for her ride one day. She was dressed for a garden party.
We're off to see the Countess. Get those horses' heads up.
My rein was tightened, and I almost couldn't bear it.
Ginger was next.
NEEIGH

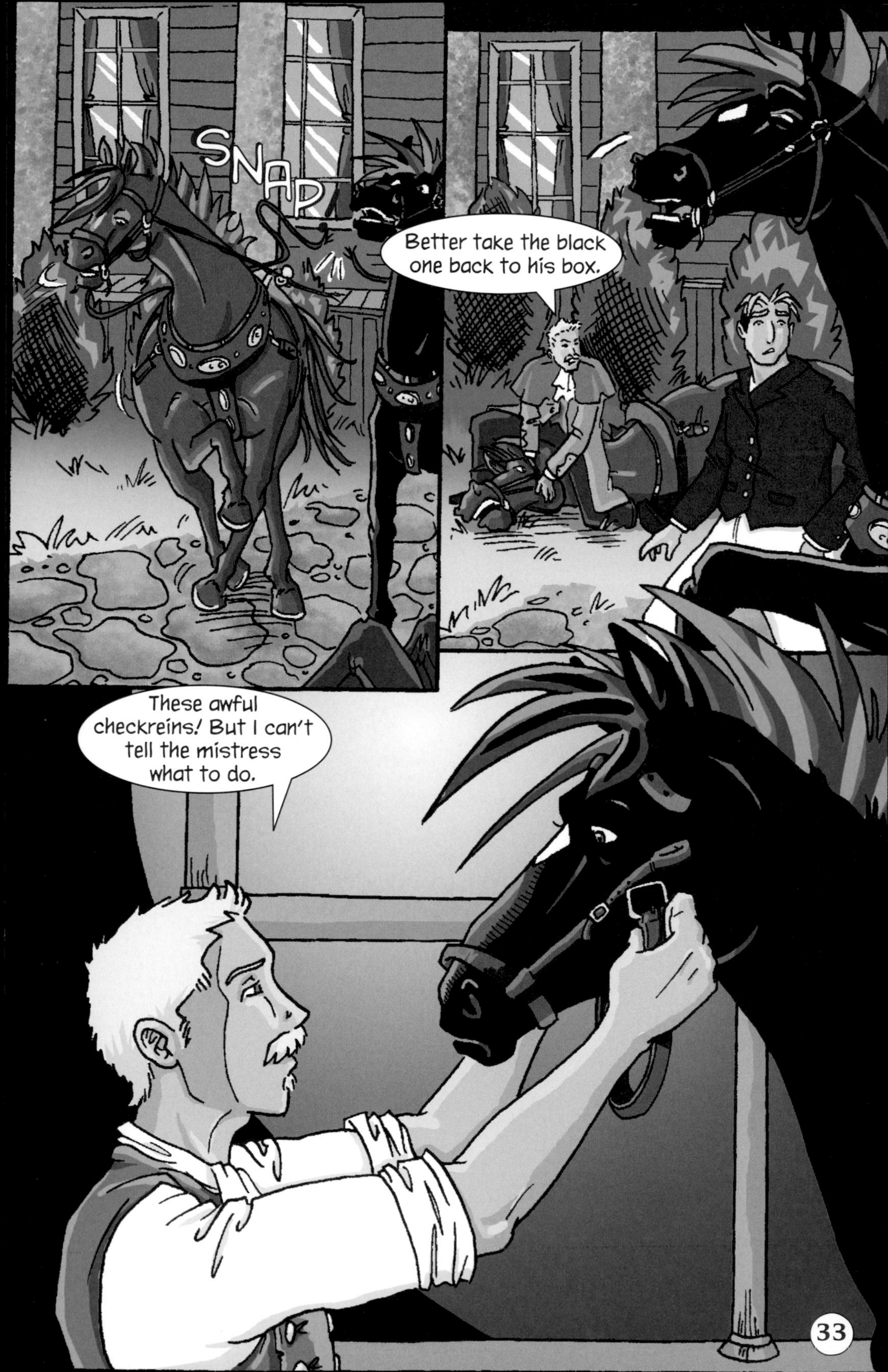
SNAP
Better take the black one back to his box.
These awful checkreins! But I can't tell the mistress what to do.

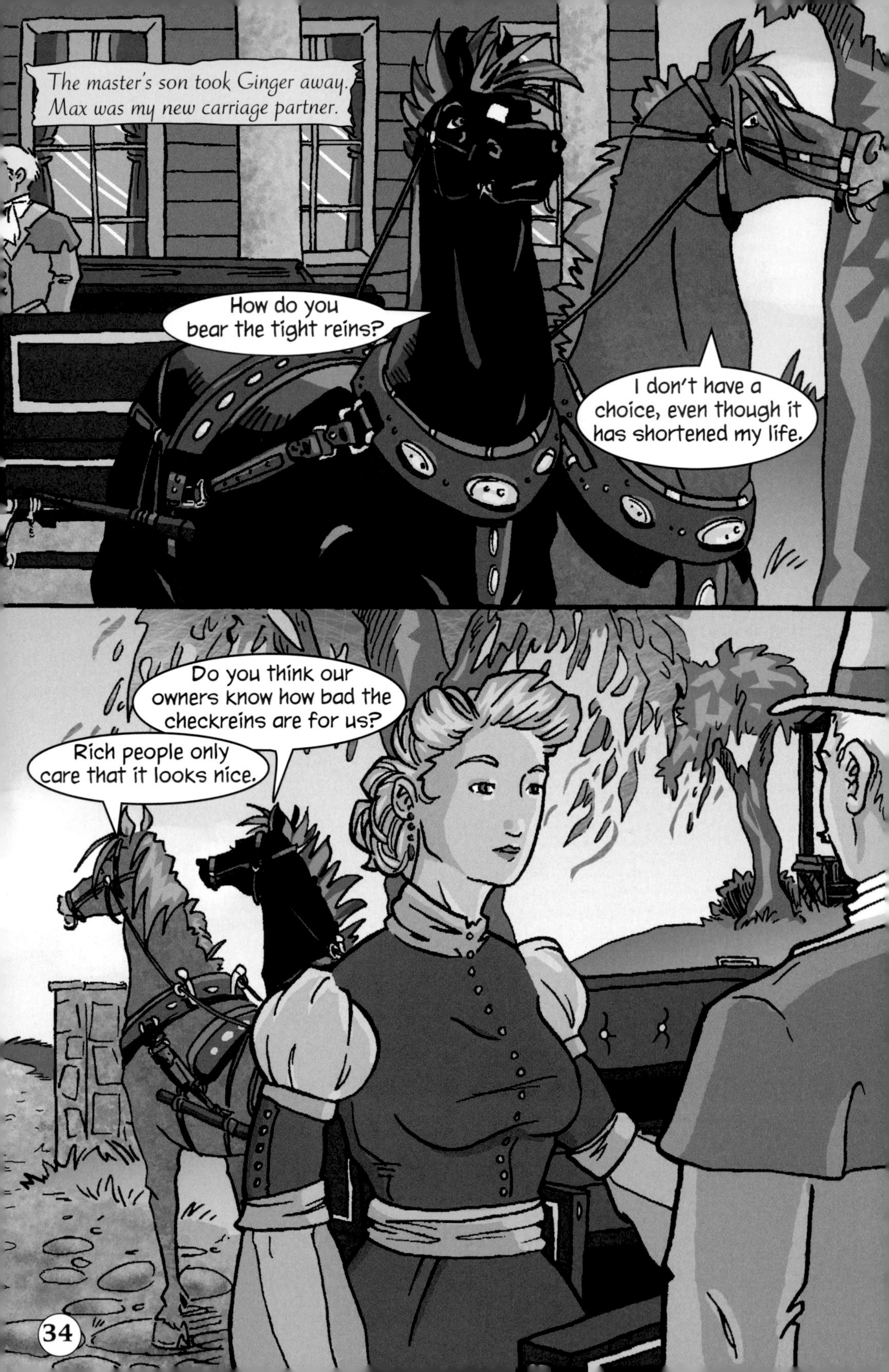

The master's son took Ginger away. Max was my new carriage partner.
How do you bear the tight reins?
I don't have a choice, even though it has shortened my life.
Do you think our owners know how bad the checkreins are for us?
Rich people only care that it looks nice.

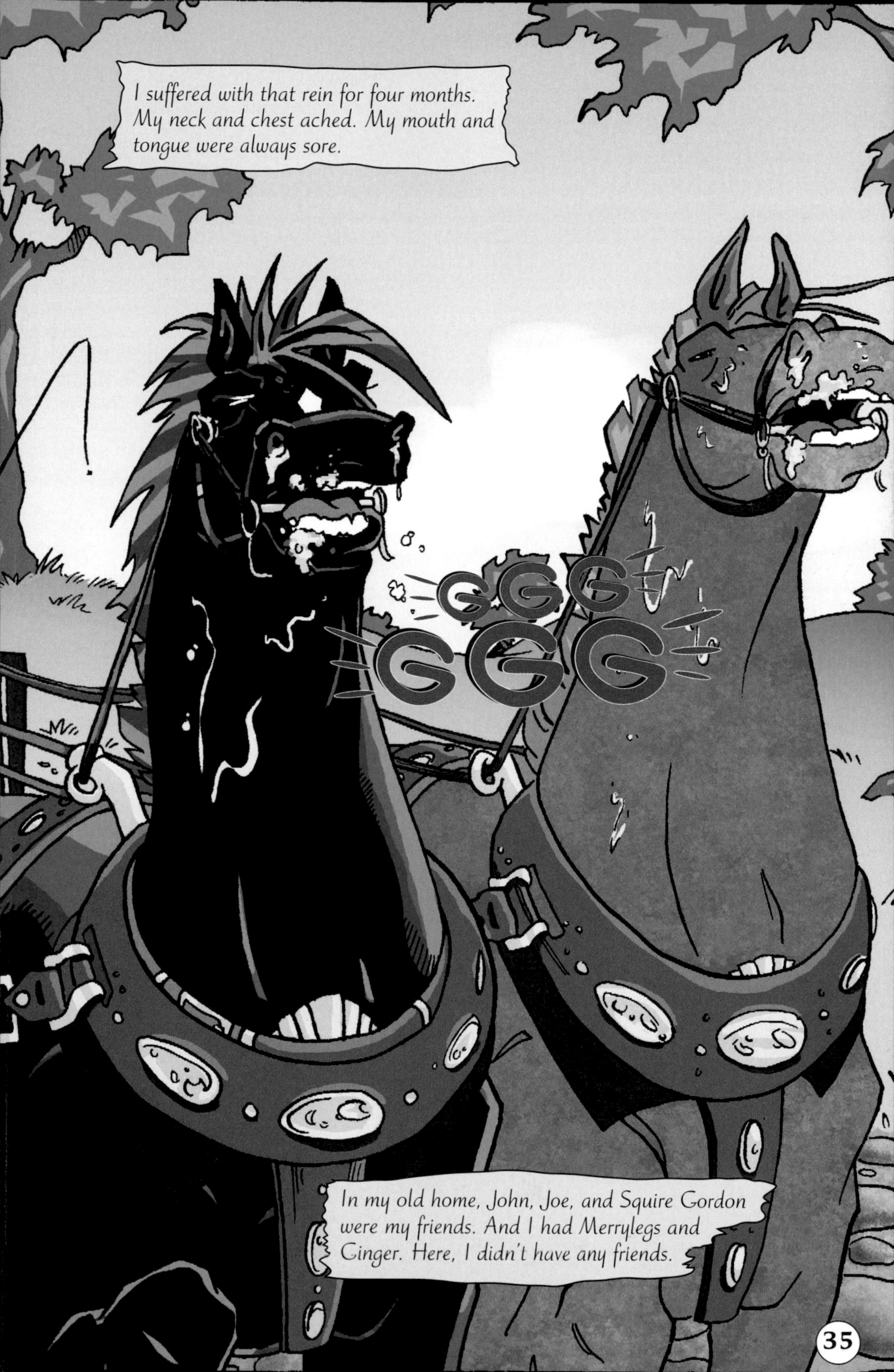

I suffered with that rein for four months. My neck and chest ached. My mouth and tongue were always sore.
GGG
GGG
In my old home, John, Joe, and Squire Gordon were my friends. And I had Merrylegs and Ginger. Here, I didn't have any friends.

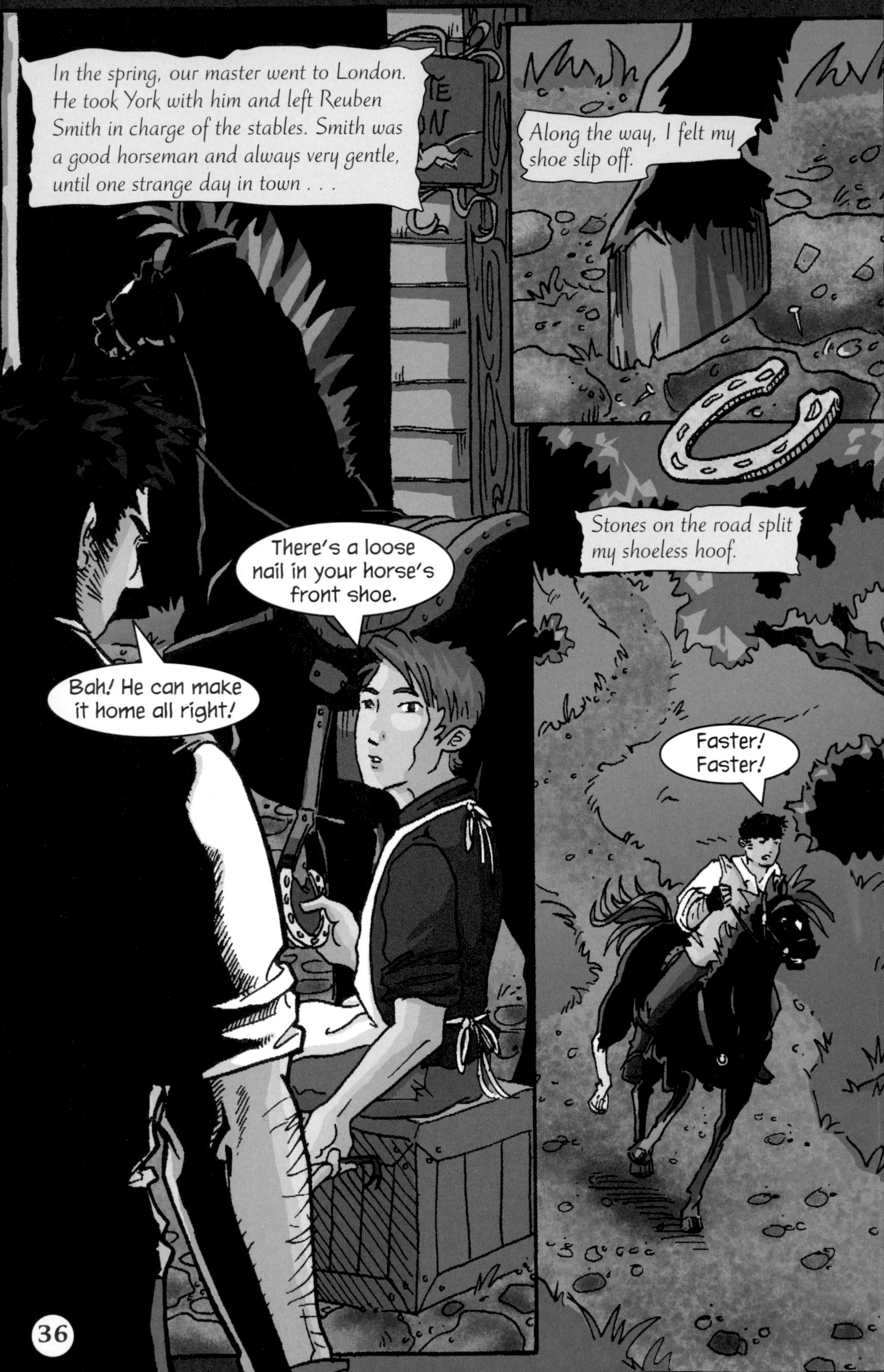
In the spring, our master went to London. He took York with him and left Reuben Smith in charge of the stables. Smith was a good horseman and always very gentle, until one strange day in town . . .
There's a loose nail in your horse's front shoe.
Bah! He can make it home all right!
Along the way, I felt my shoe slip off.
Stones on the road split my shoeless hoof.
Faster! Faster!

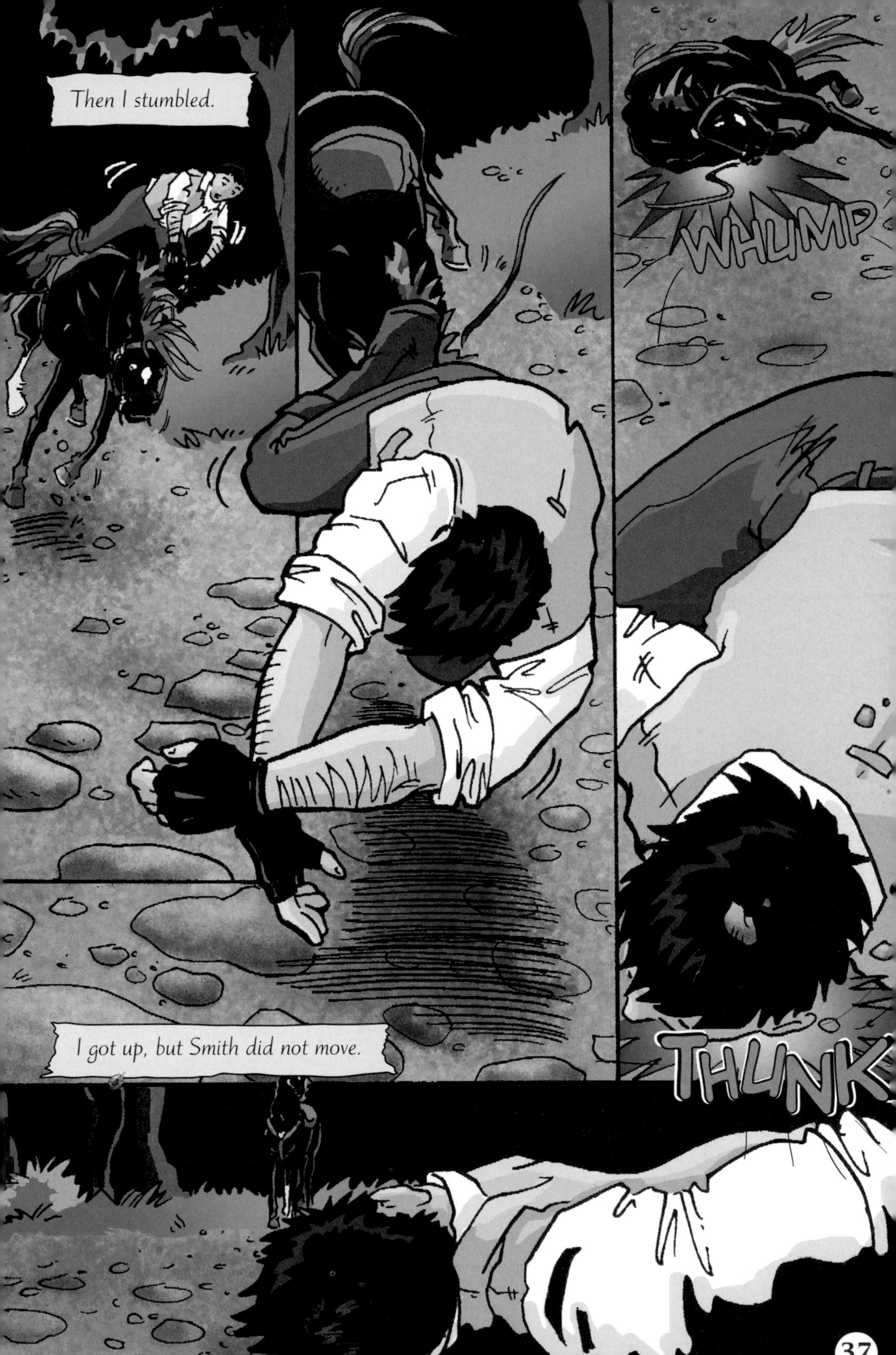
Then I stumbled.
WHUMP
I got up, but Smith did not move.
THUNK

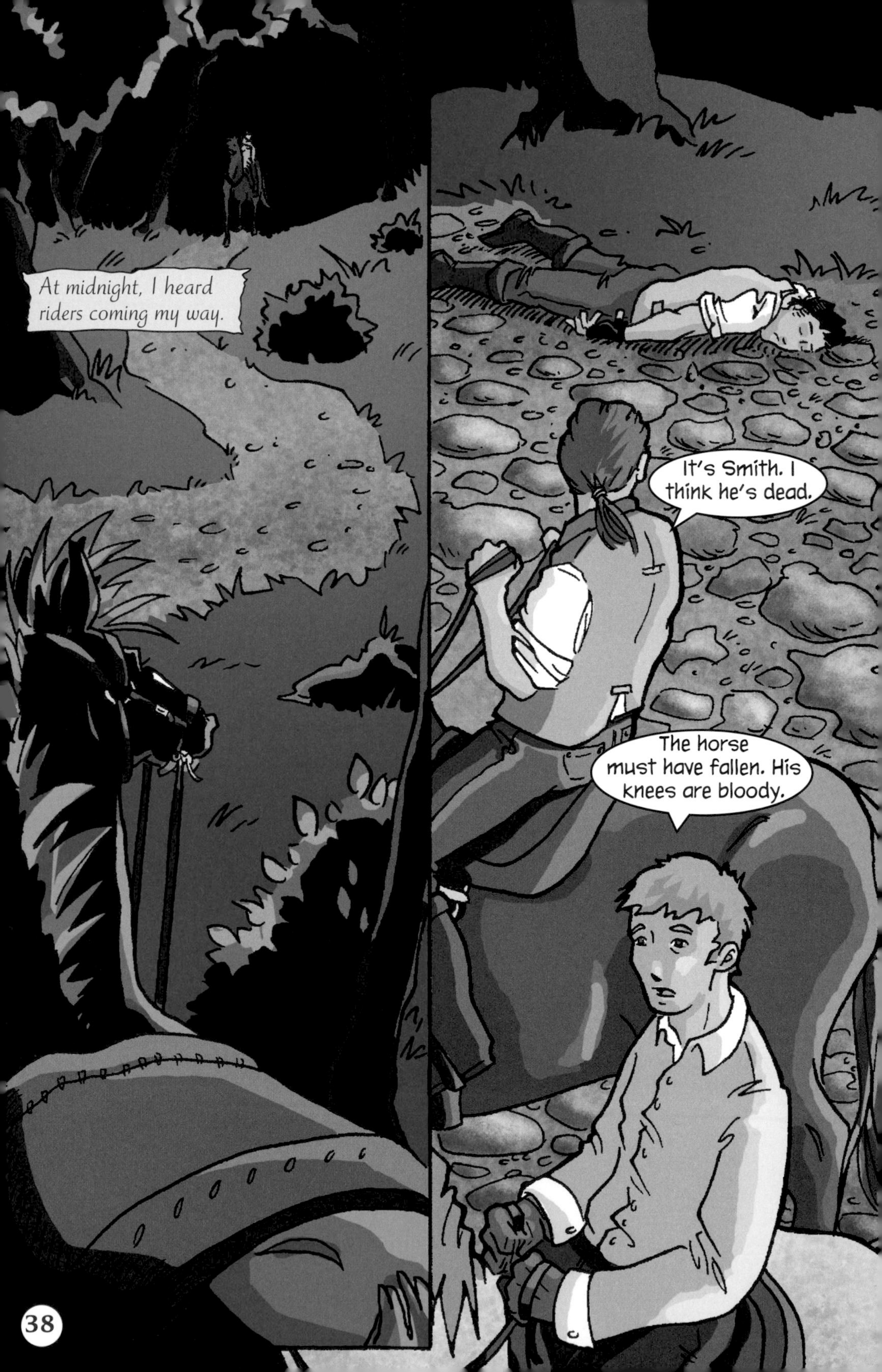
At midnight, I heard riders coming my way.
It's Smith. I think he's dead.
The horse must have fallen. His knees are bloody.

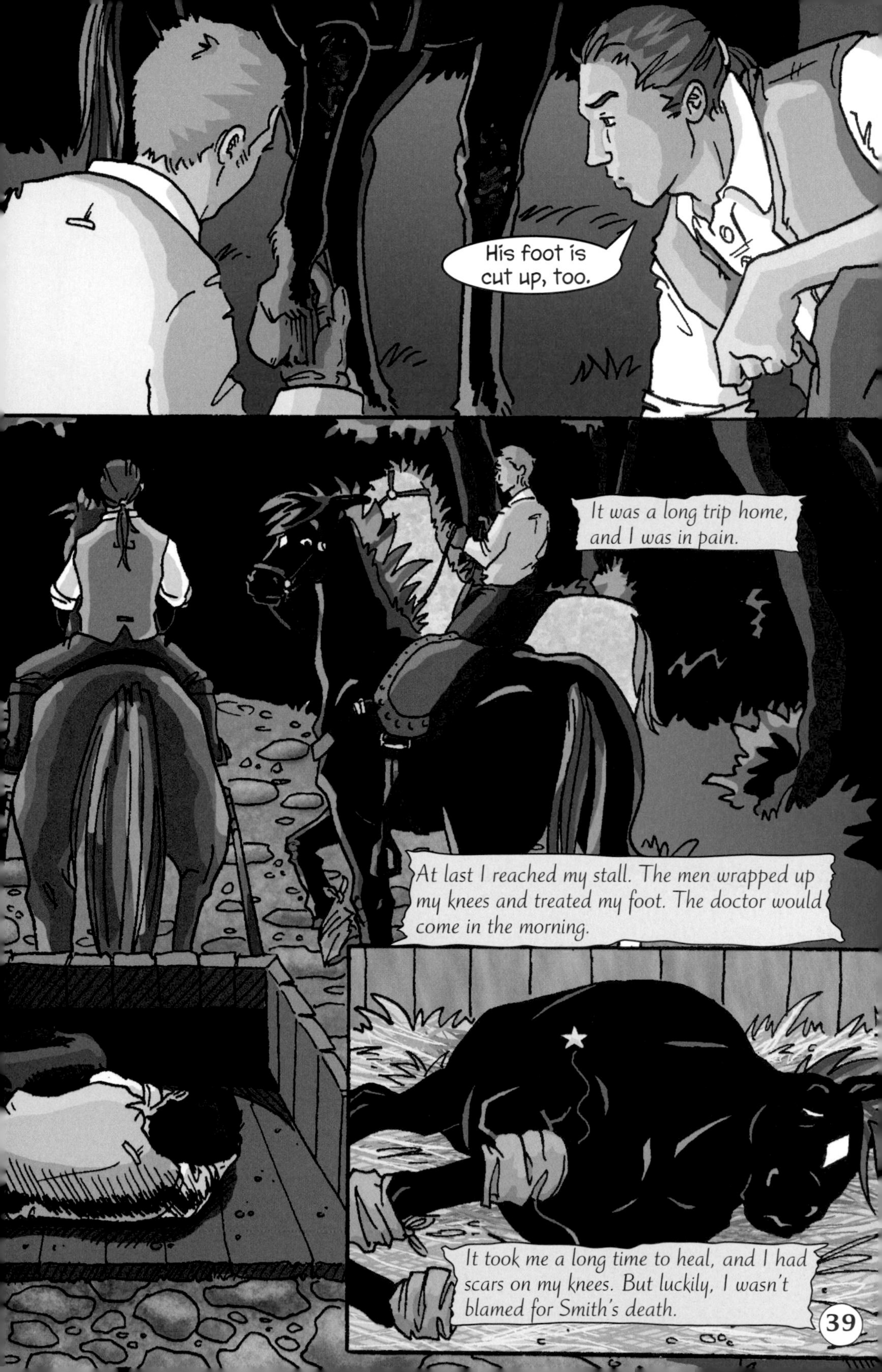

His foot is cut up, too.
It was a long trip home, and I was in pain.
At last I reached my stall. The men wrapped up my knees and treated my foot. The doctor would come in the morning.
It took me a long time to heal, and I had scars on my knees. But luckily, I wasn't blamed for Smith's death.

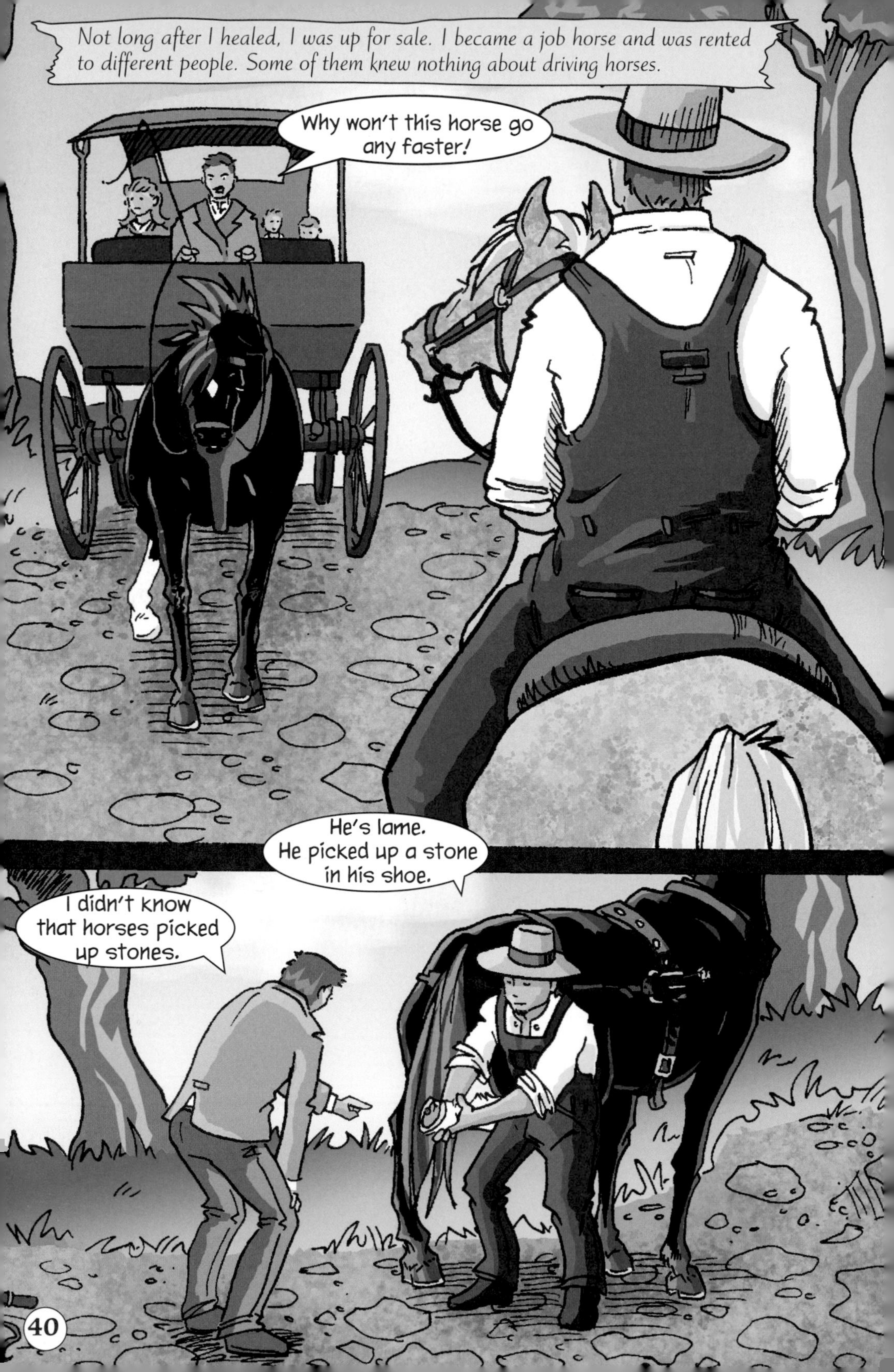
Not long after I healed, I was up for sale. I became a job horse and was rented to different people. Some of them knew nothing about driving horses.
Why won't this horse go any faster!
He's lame. He picked up a stone in his shoe.
I didn't know that horses picked up stones.

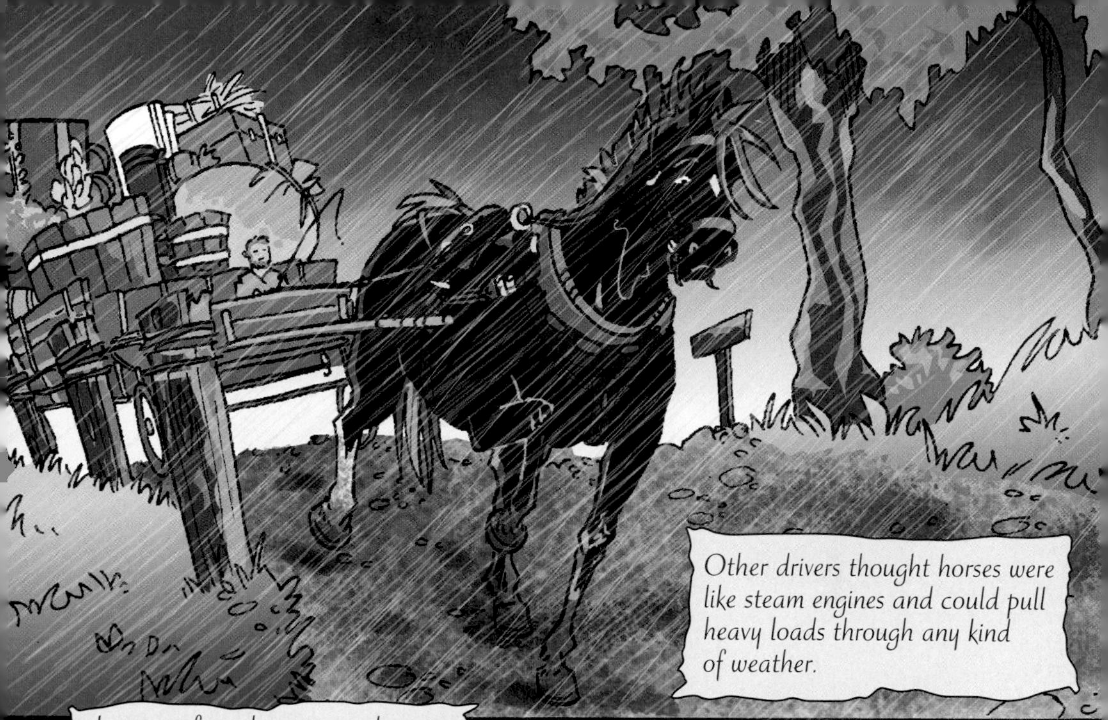
Other drivers thought horses were like steam engines and could pull heavy loads through any kind of weather.

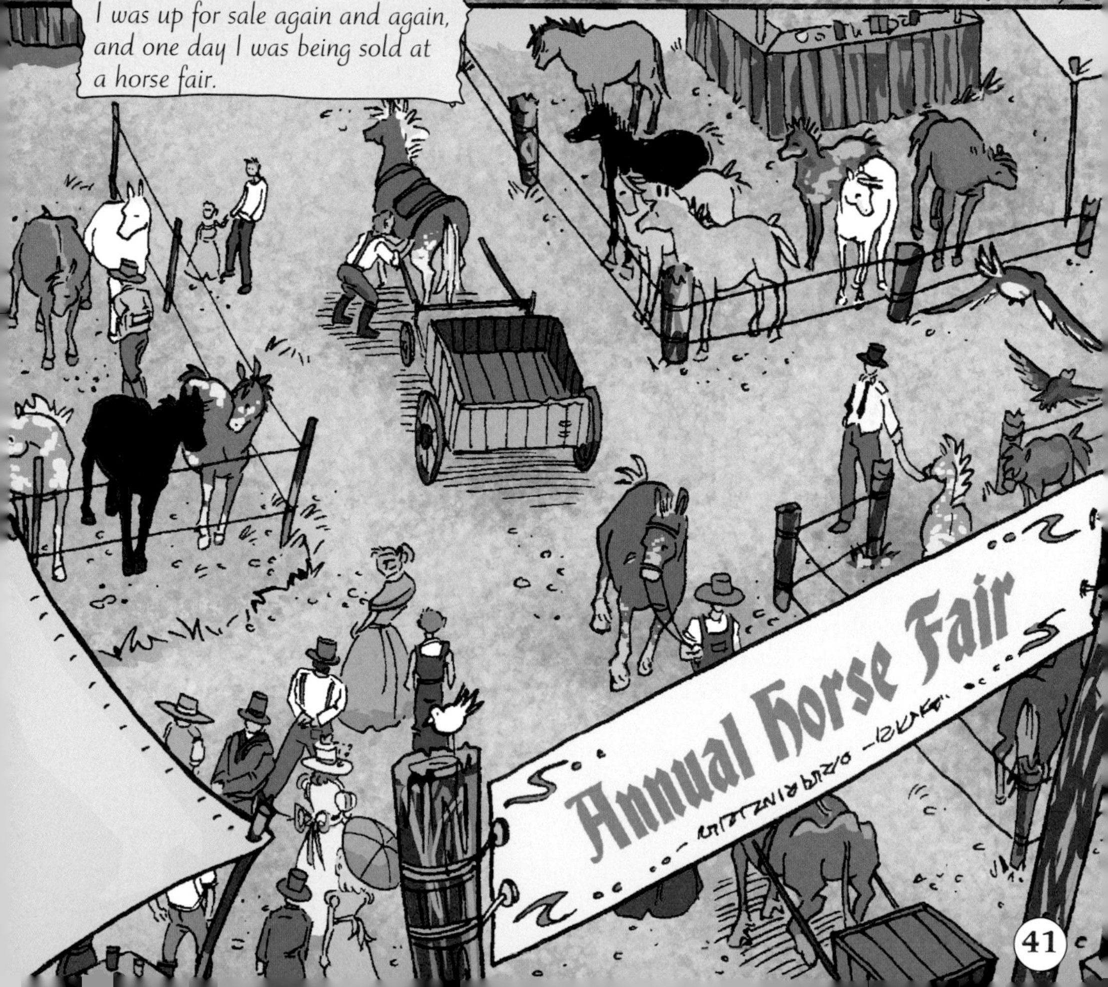
I was up for sale again and again, and one day I was being sold at a horse fair.
Annual Horse Fair

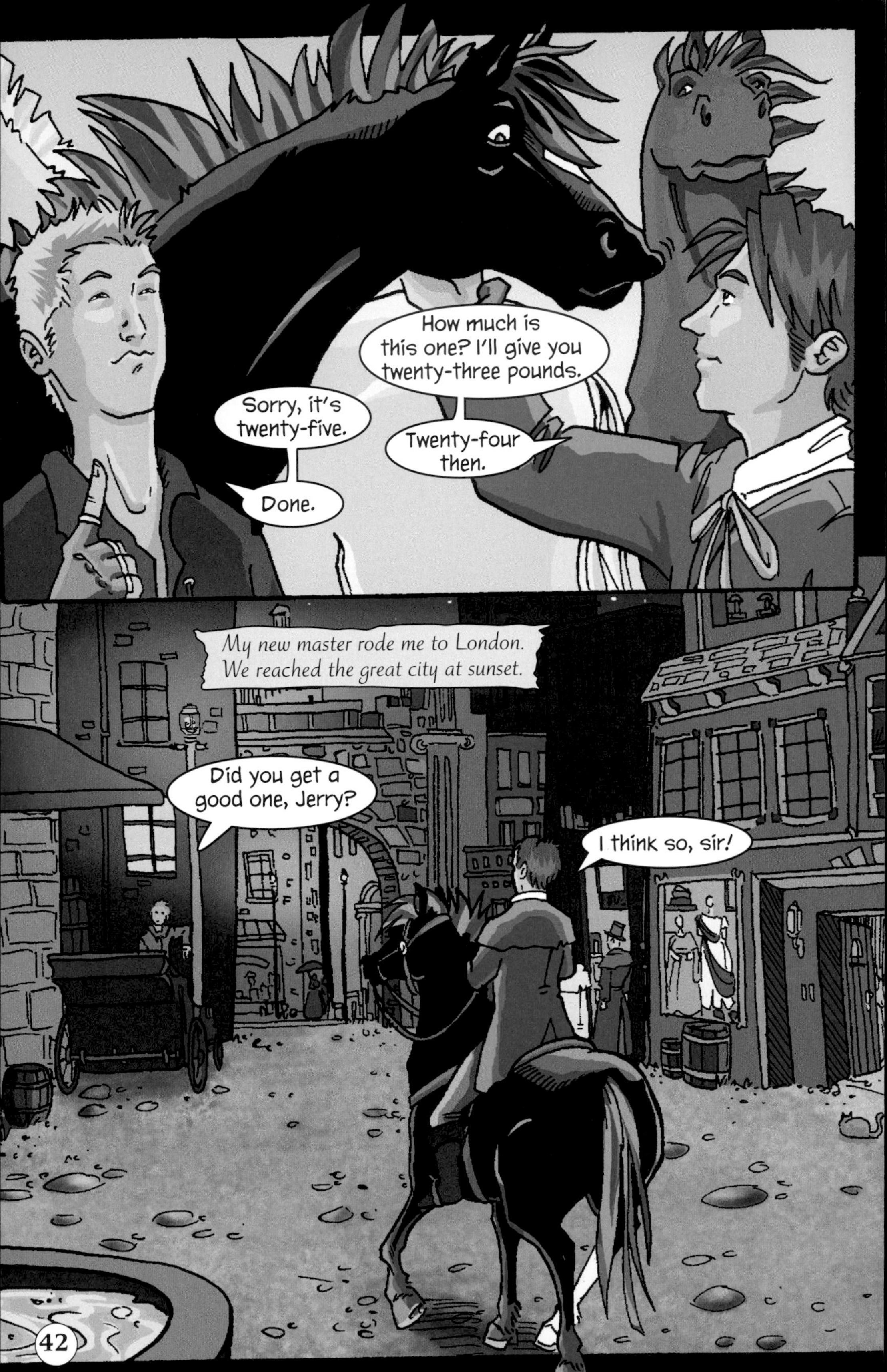
How much is this one? I'll give you twenty-three pounds.
Sorry, it's twenty-five.
Twenty-four then.
Done.
My new master rode me to London. We reached the great city at sunset.
Did you get a good one, Jerry?
I think so, sir!

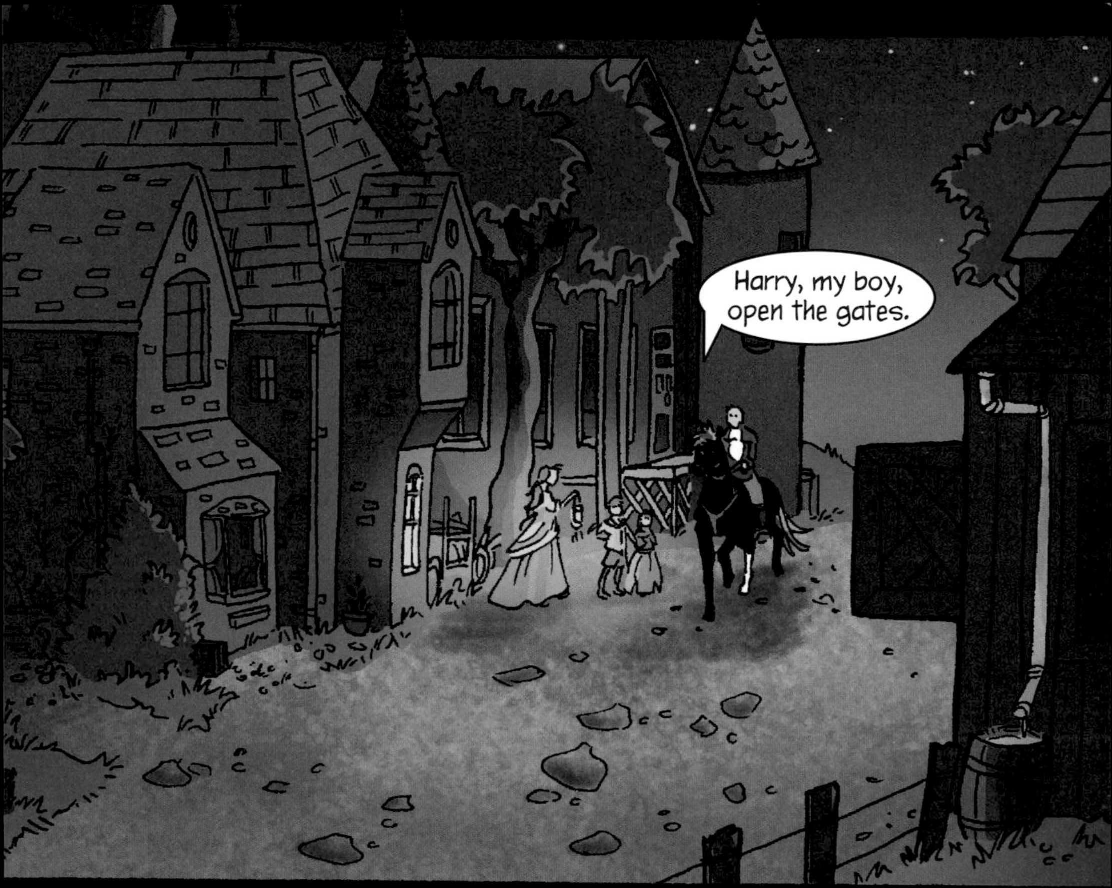
Harry, my boy, open the gates.

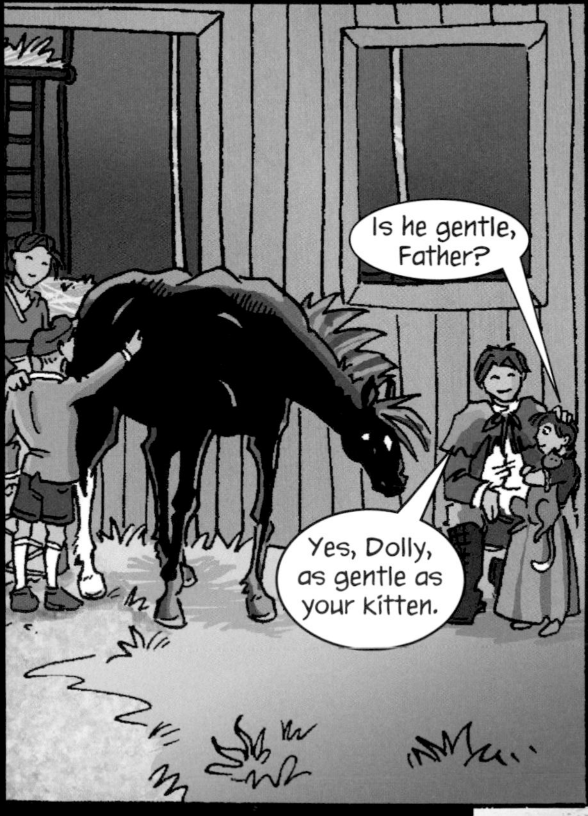
Is he gentle, Father?
Yes, Dolly, as gentle as your kitten.

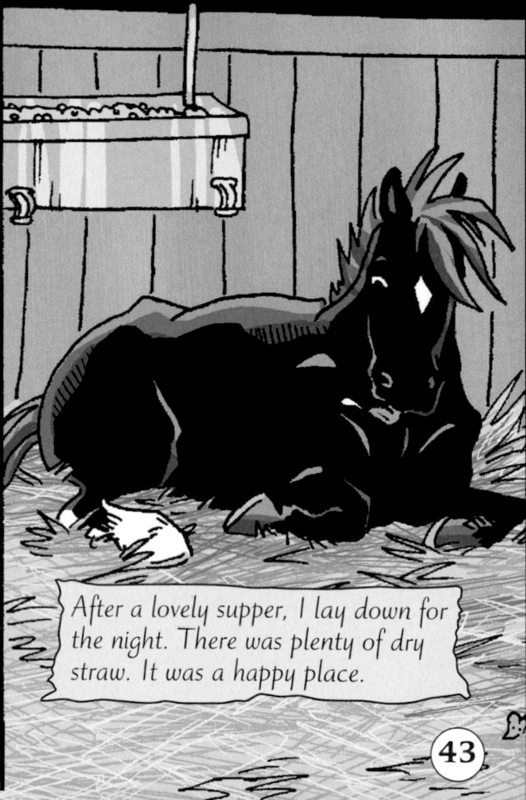
After a lovely supper, I lay down for the night. There was plenty of dry straw. It was a happy place.

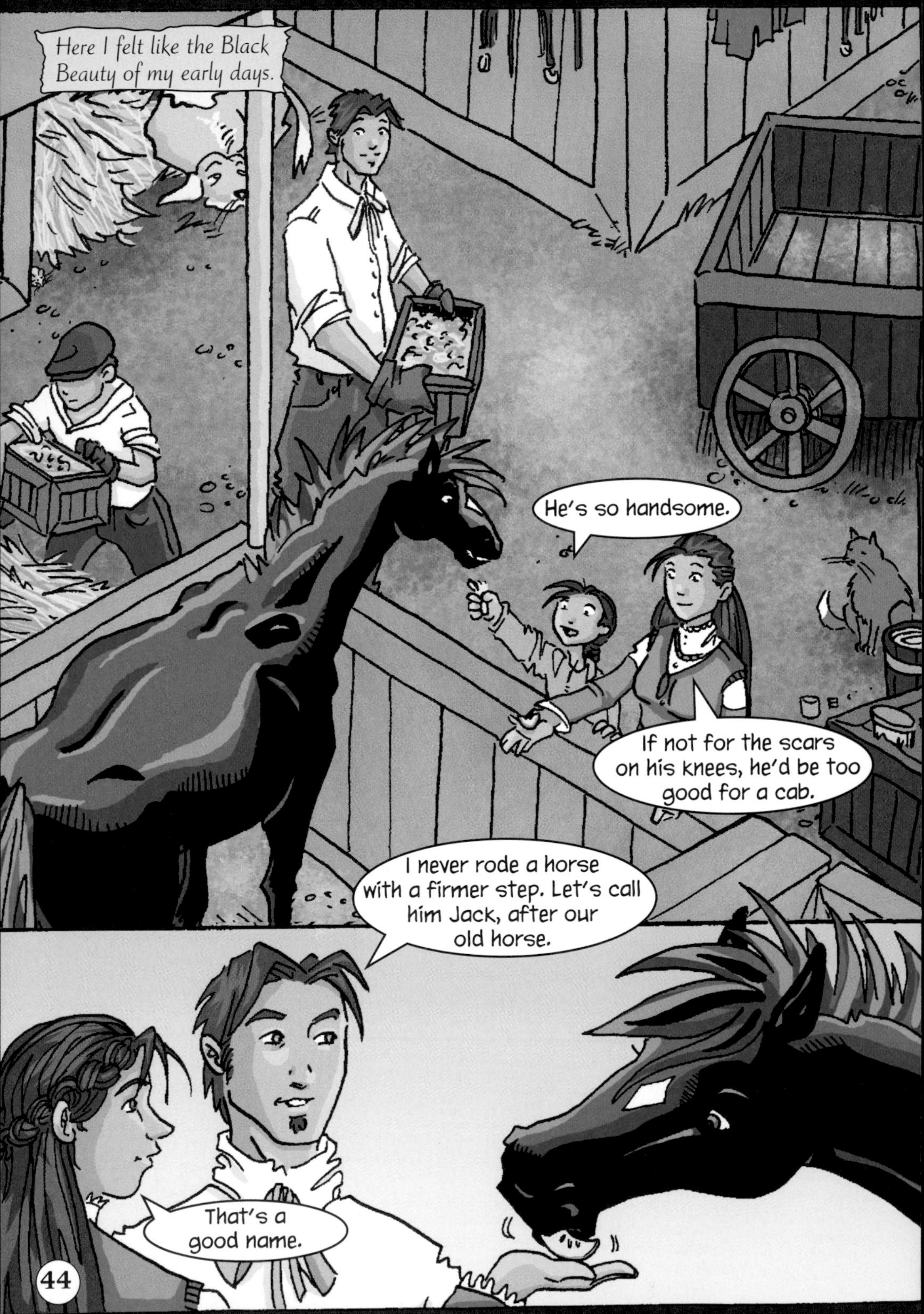
Here I felt like the Black Beauty of my early days.
He's so handsome.
If not for the scars on his knees, he'd be too good for a cab.
I never rode a horse with a firmer step. Let's call him Jack, after our old horse.
That's a good name.

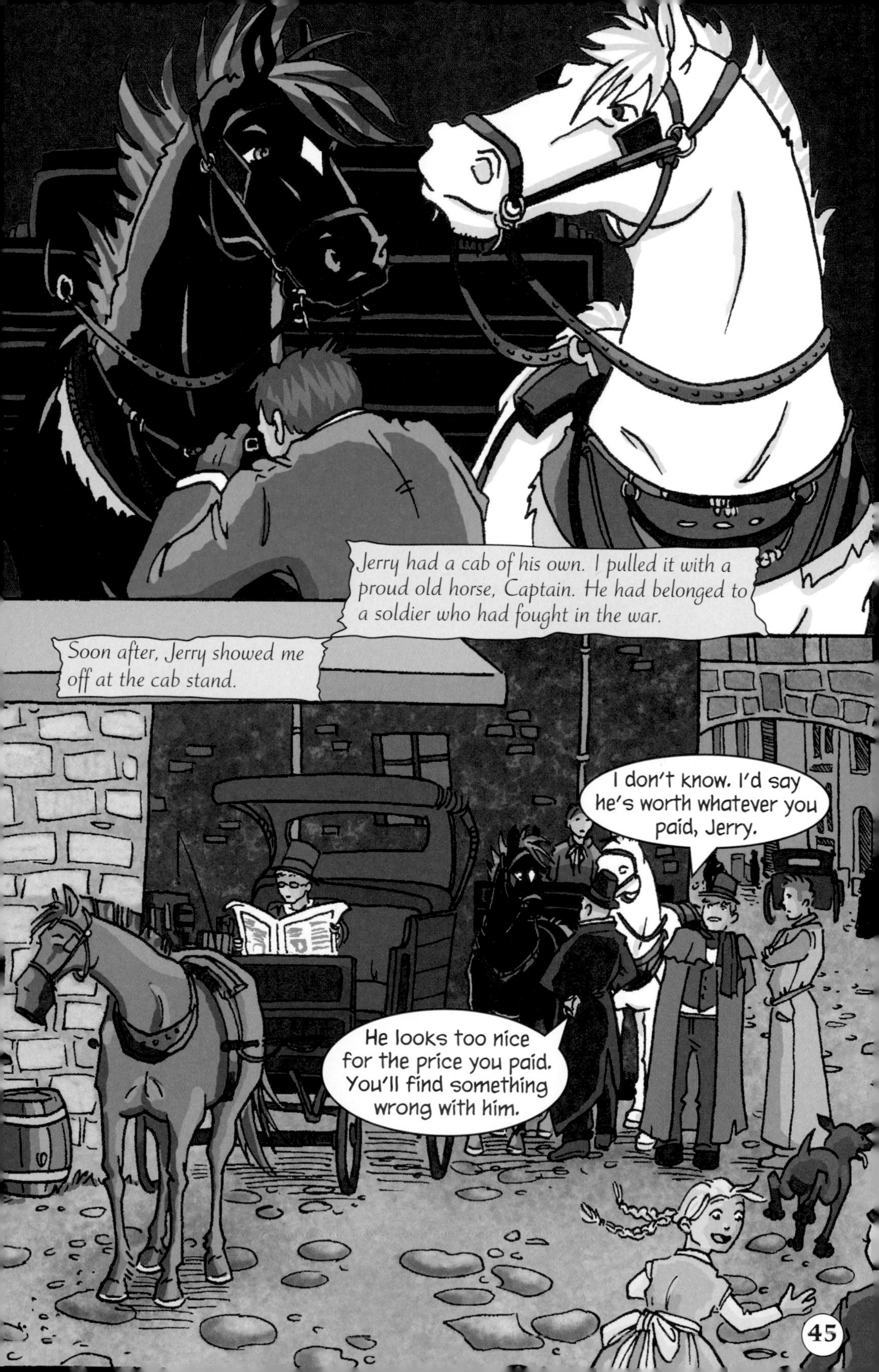

Jerry had a cab of his own. I pulled it with a proud old horse, Captain. He had belonged to a soldier who had fought in the war.
Soon after, Jerry showed me off at the cab stand.
I don't know. I'd say he's worth whatever you paid, Jerry.
He looks too nice for the price you paid. You'll find something wrong with him.

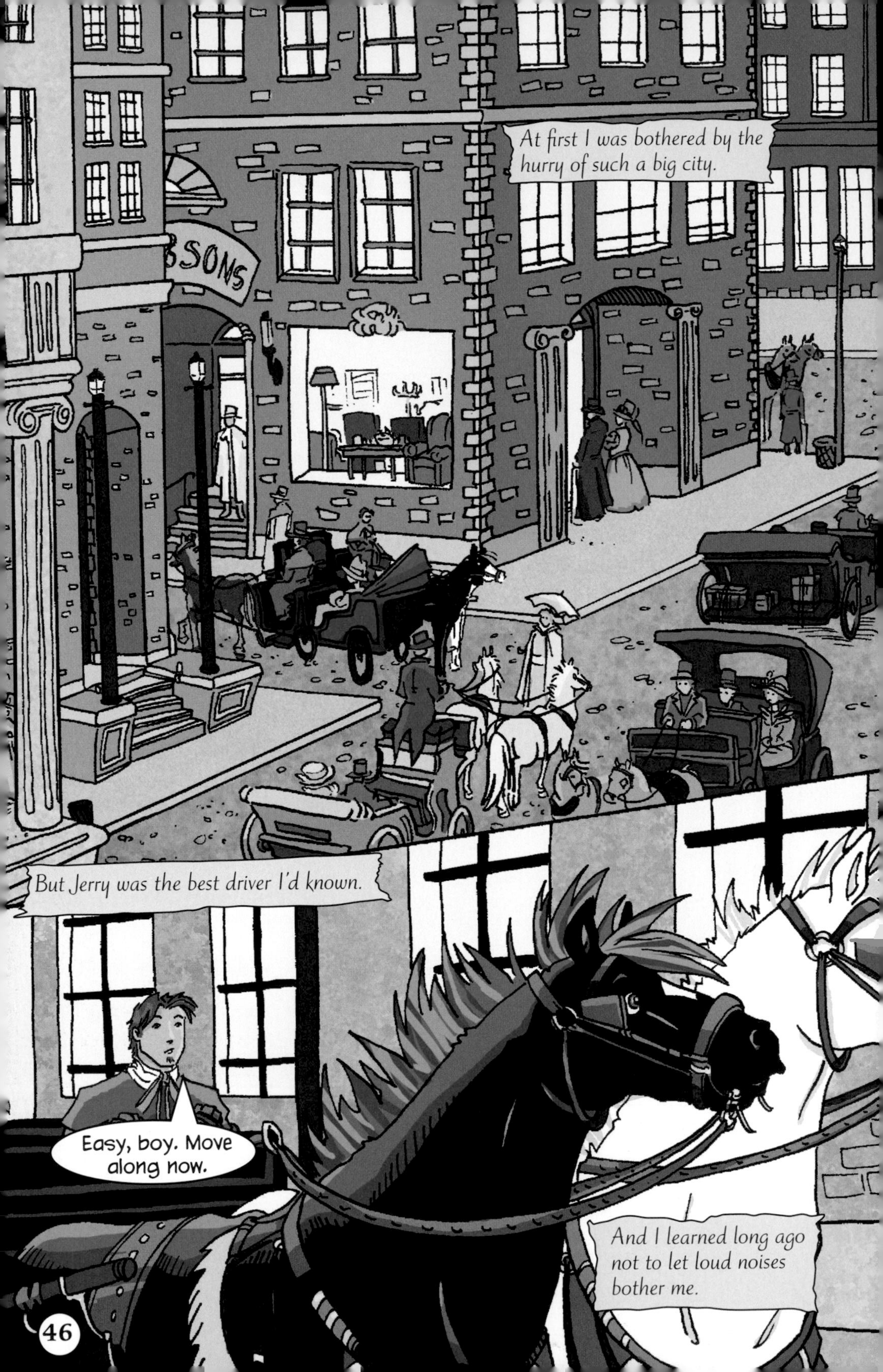
BSONS
At first I was bothered by the hurry of such a big city.
But Jerry was the best driver I'd known.
Easy, boy. Move along now.
And I learned long ago not to let loud noises bother me.

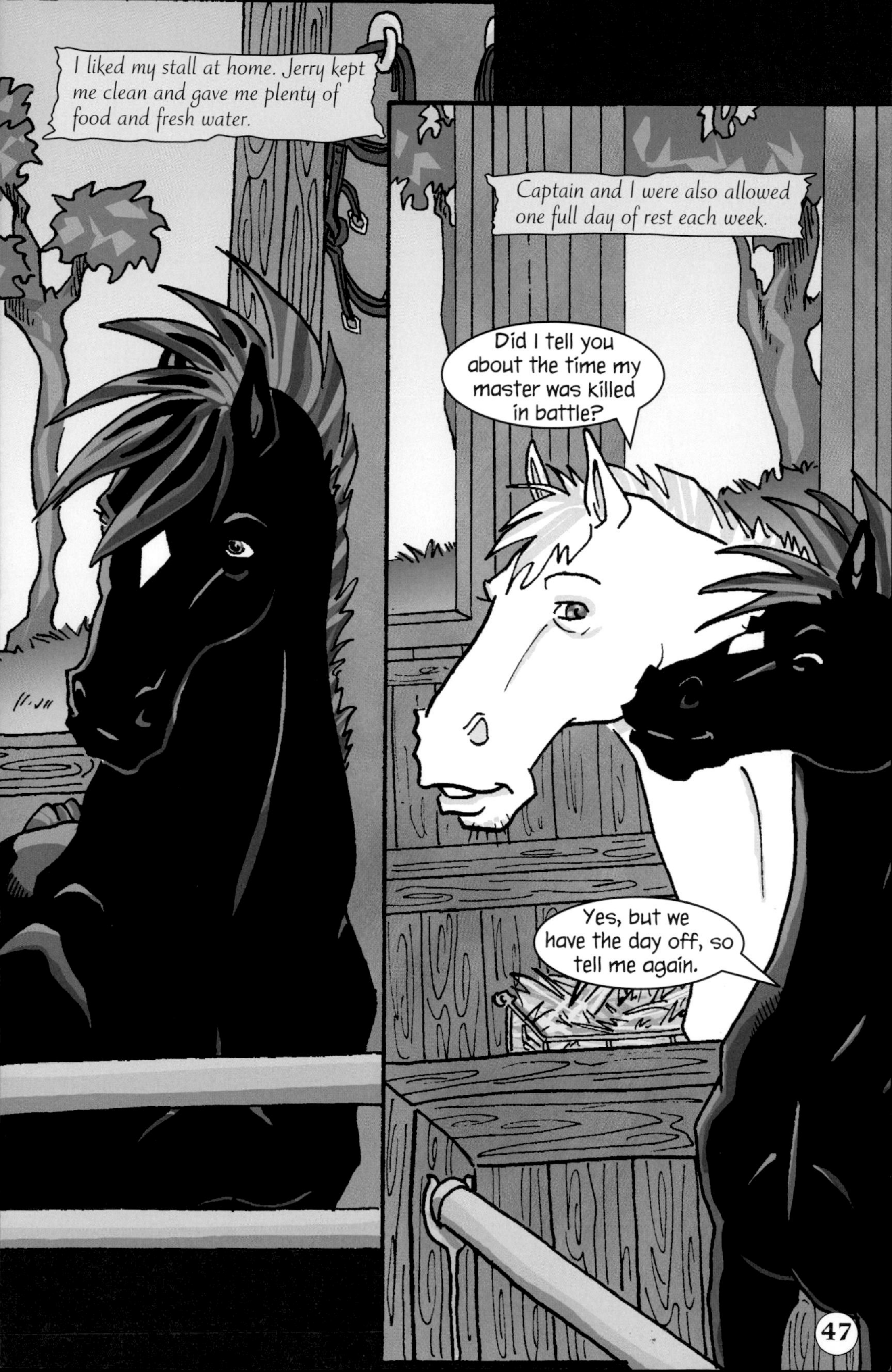
I liked my stall at home. Jerry kept me clean and gave me plenty of food and fresh water.
Captain and I were also allowed one full day of rest each week.
Did I tell you about the time my master was killed in battle?
Yes, but we have the day off, so tell me again.

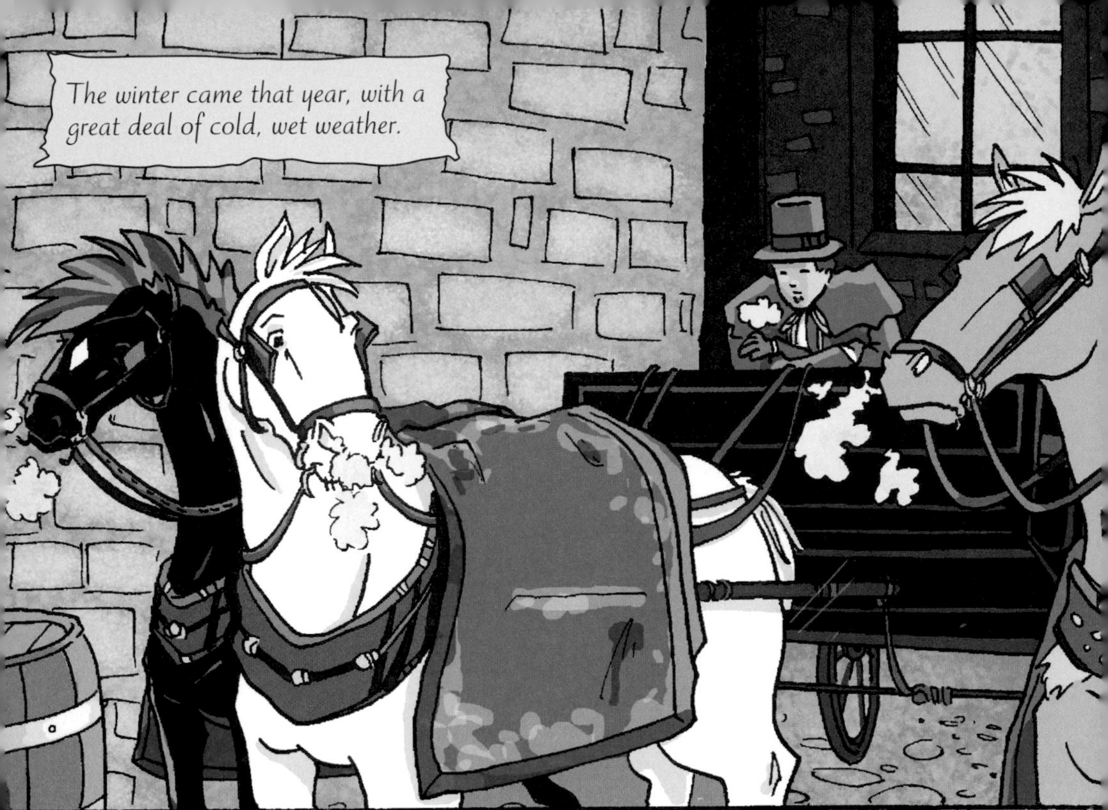
The winter came that year, with a great deal of cold, wet weather.

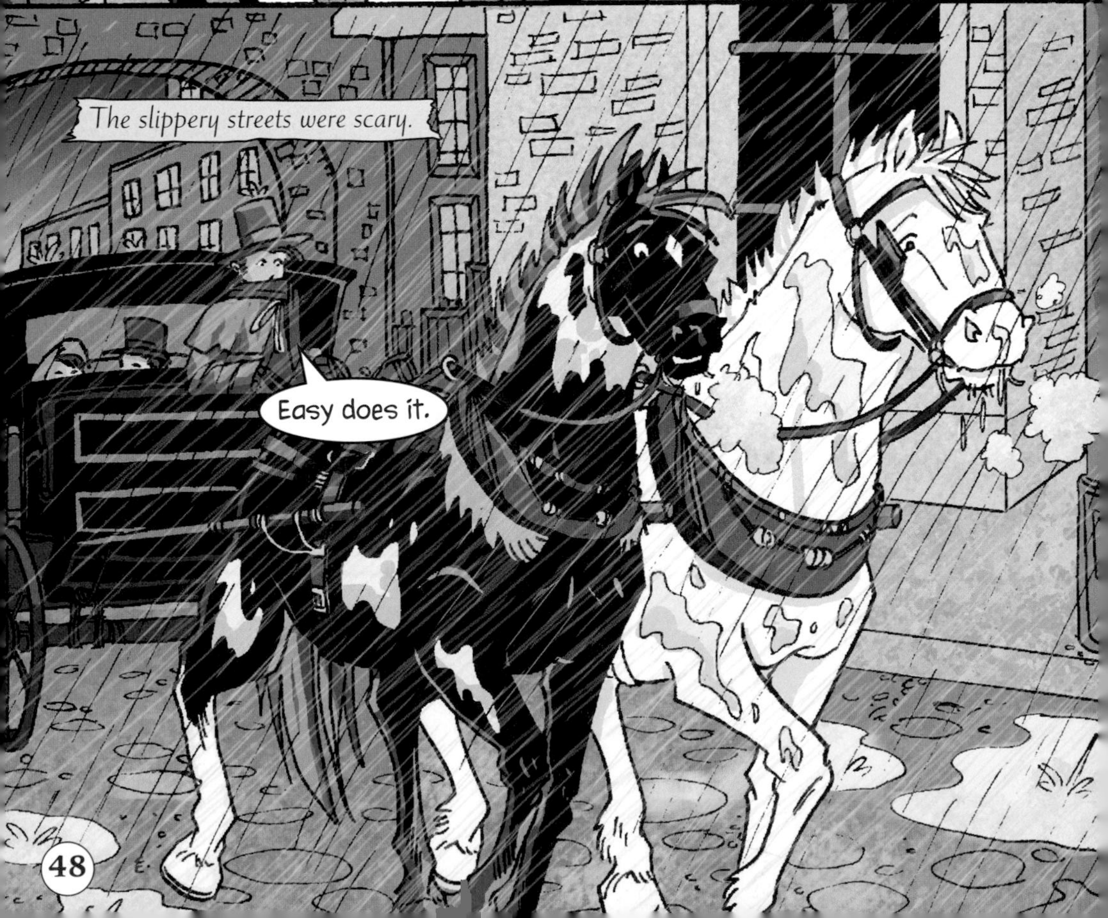
The slippery streets were scary.
Easy does it.

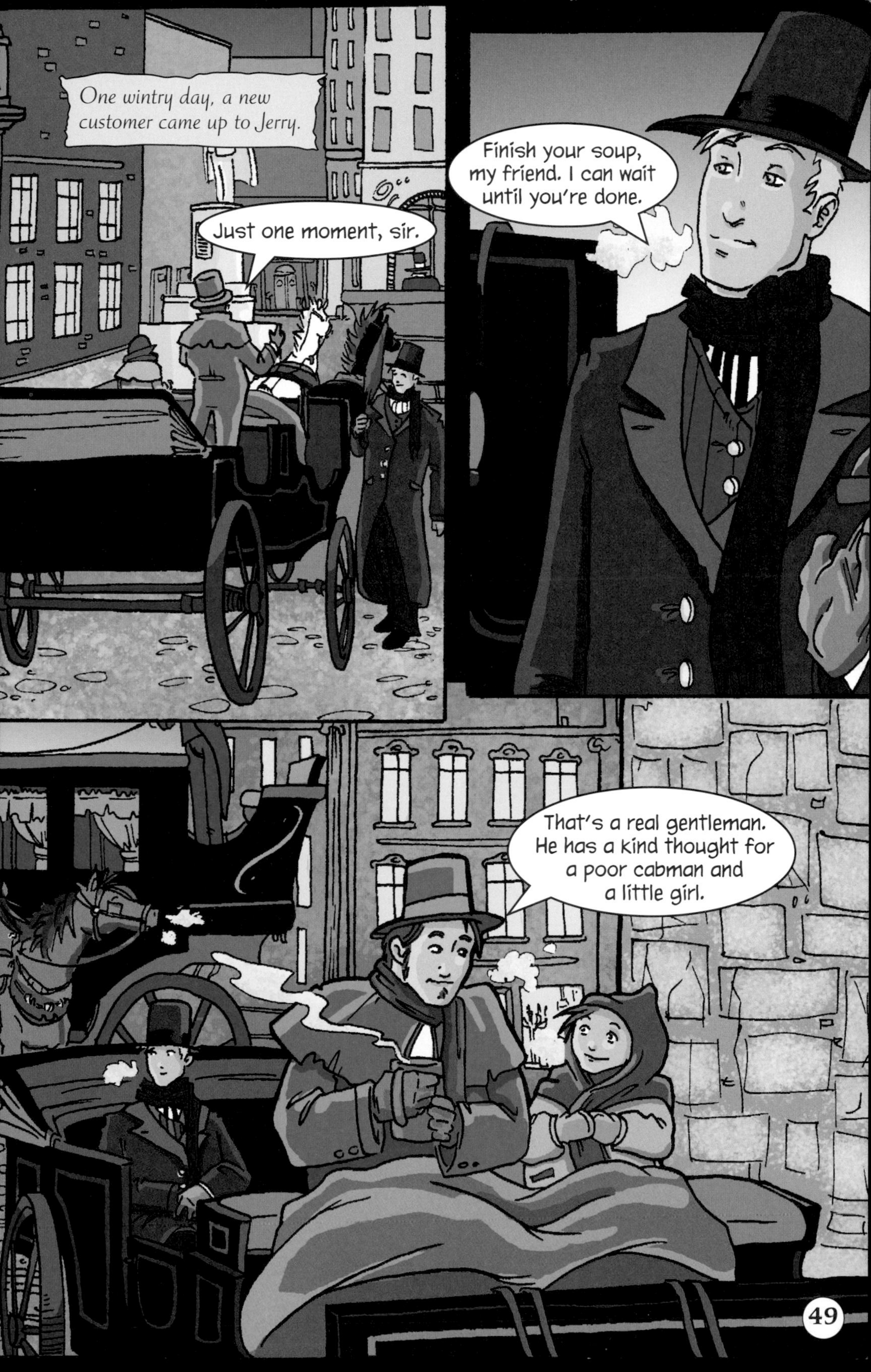
One wintry day, a new customer came up to Jerry.
Just one moment, sir.
Finish your soup, my friend. I can wait until you're done.
That's a real gentleman. He has a kind thought for a poor cabman and a little girl.

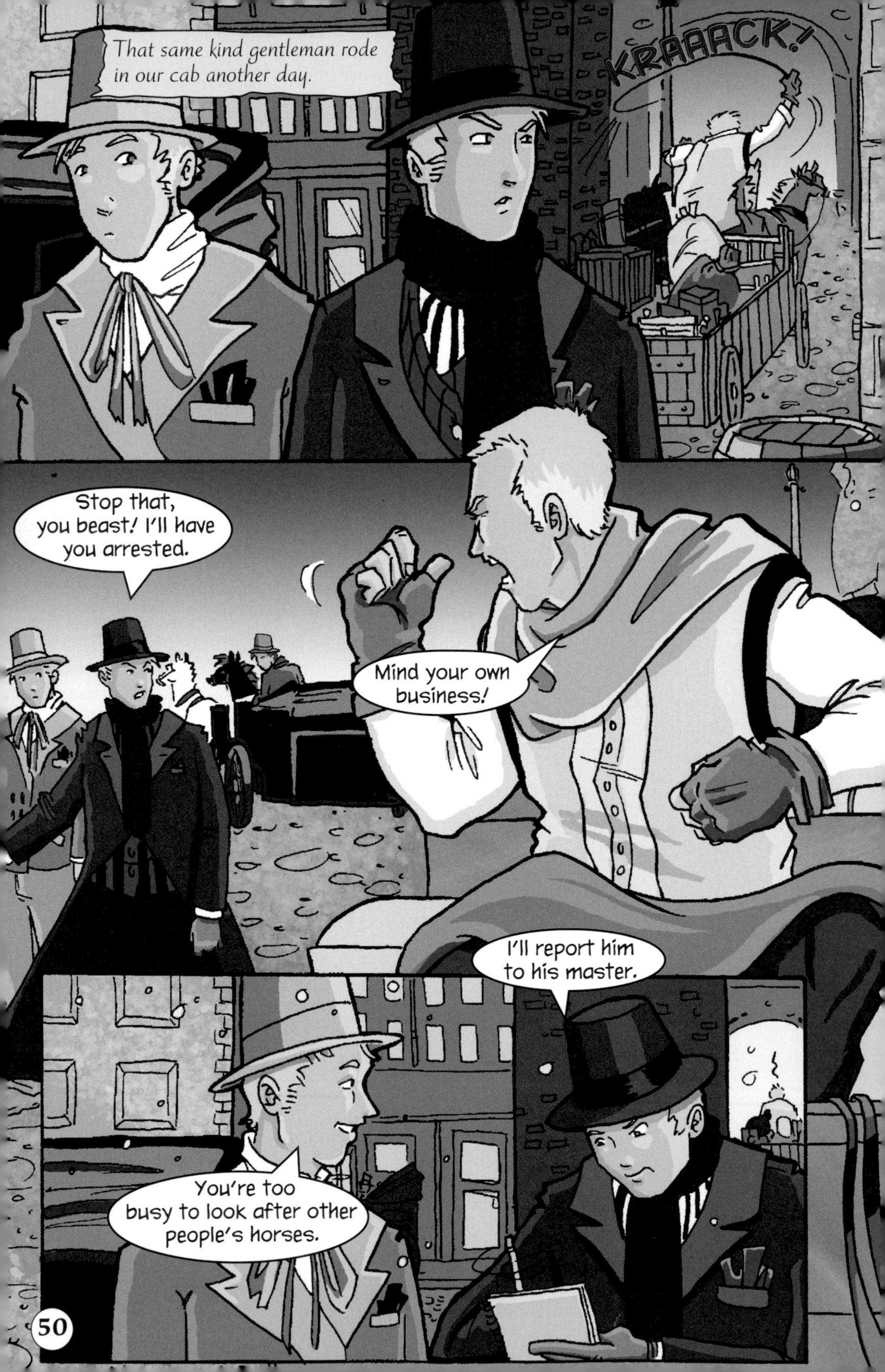
That same kind gentleman rode in our cab another day.
KRAAACK!
Stop that, you beast! I'll have you arrested.
Mind your own business!
I'll report him to his master.
You're too busy to look after other people's horses.

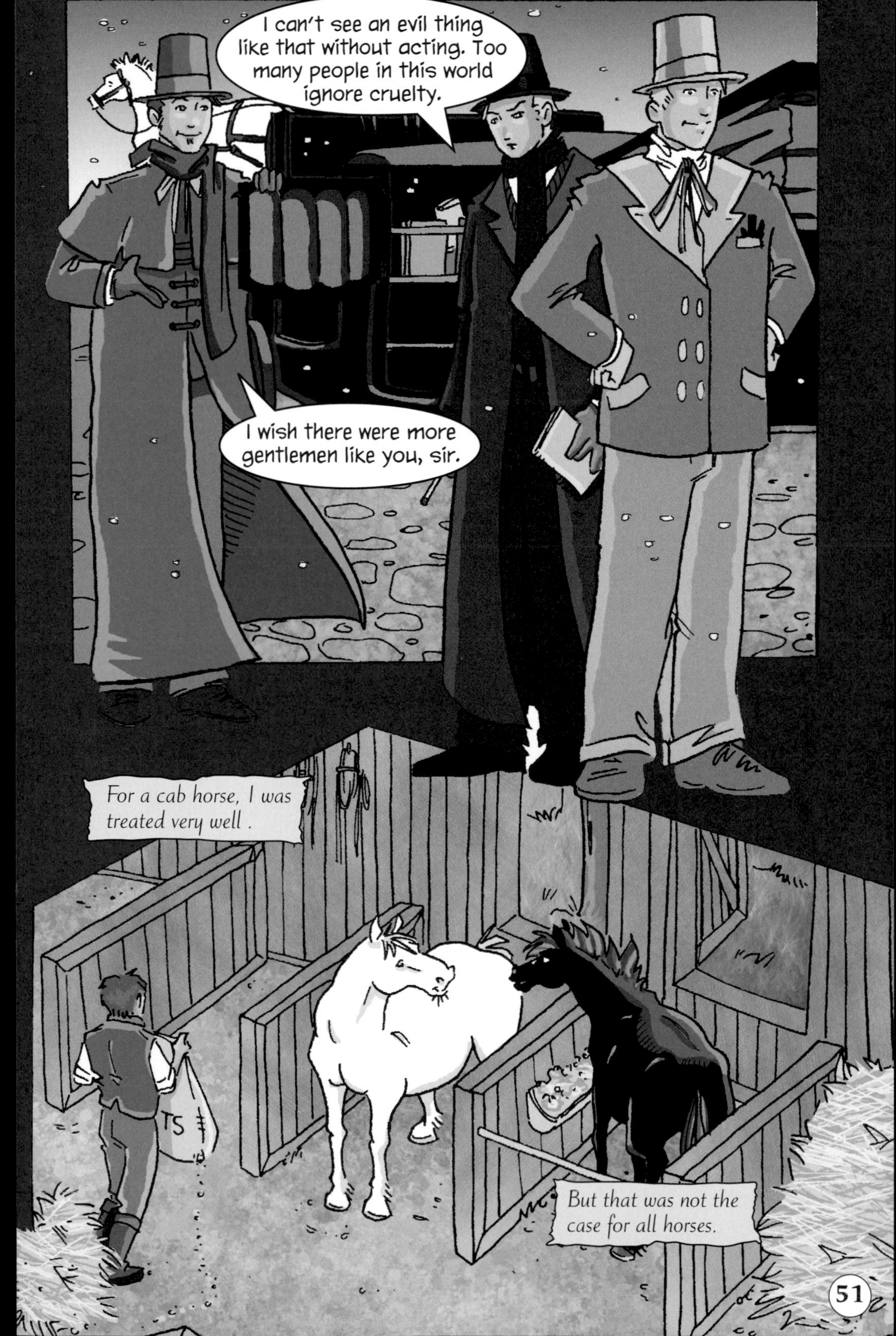
I can't see an evil thing like that without acting. Too many people in this world ignore cruelty.
I wish there were more gentlemen like you, sir.
For a cab horse, I was treated very well .
TS
But that was not the case for all horses.

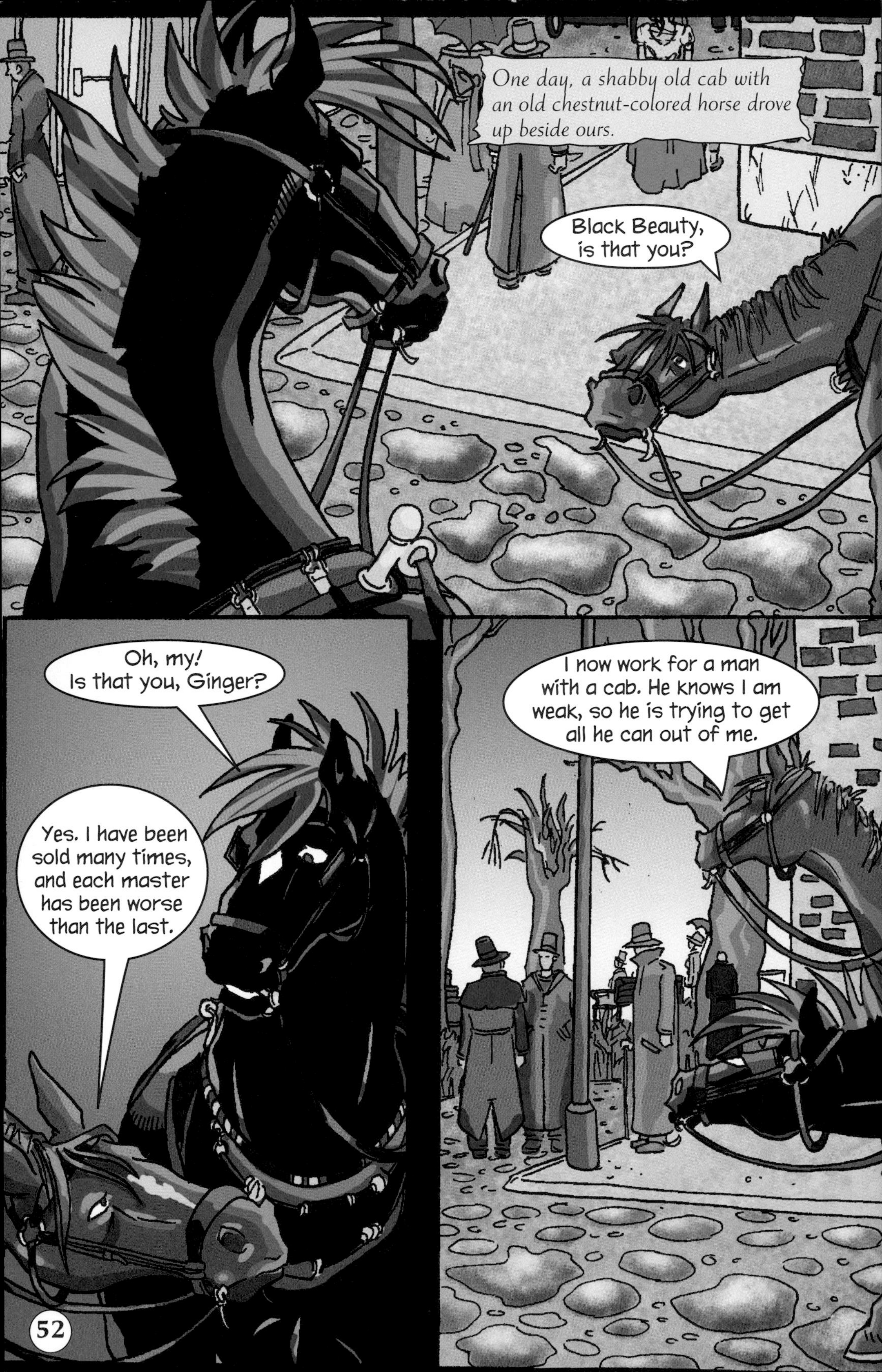
One day, a shabby old cab with an old chestnut-colored horse drove up beside ours.
Black Beauty, is that you?
Oh, my! Is that you, Ginger?
Yes. I have been sold many times, and each master has been worse than the last.
I now work for a man with a cab. He knows I am weak, so he is trying to get all he can out of me.

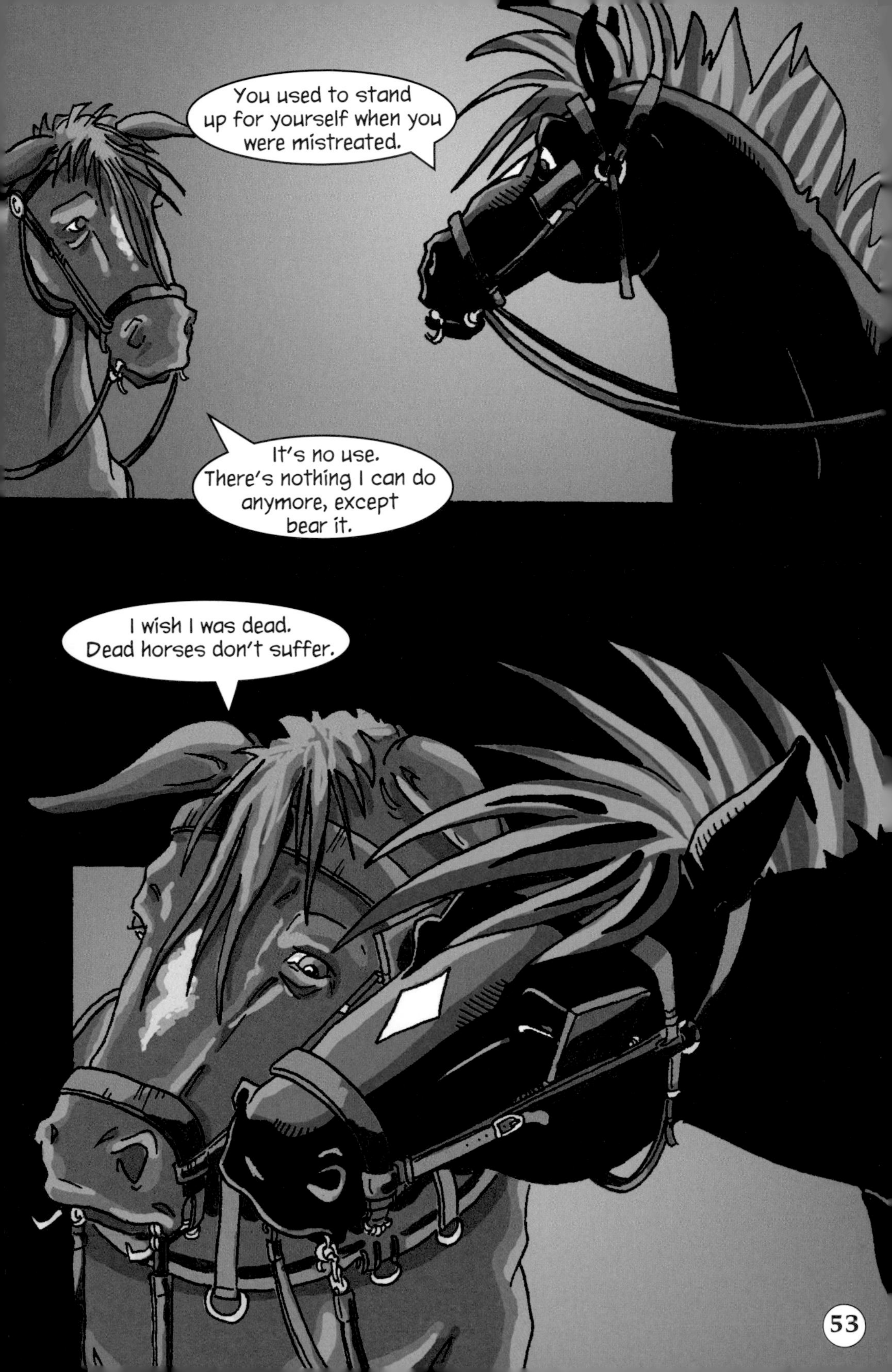
You used to stand up for yourself when you were mistreated.
It's no use. There's nothing I can do anymore, except bear it.
I wish I was dead. Dead horses don't suffer.

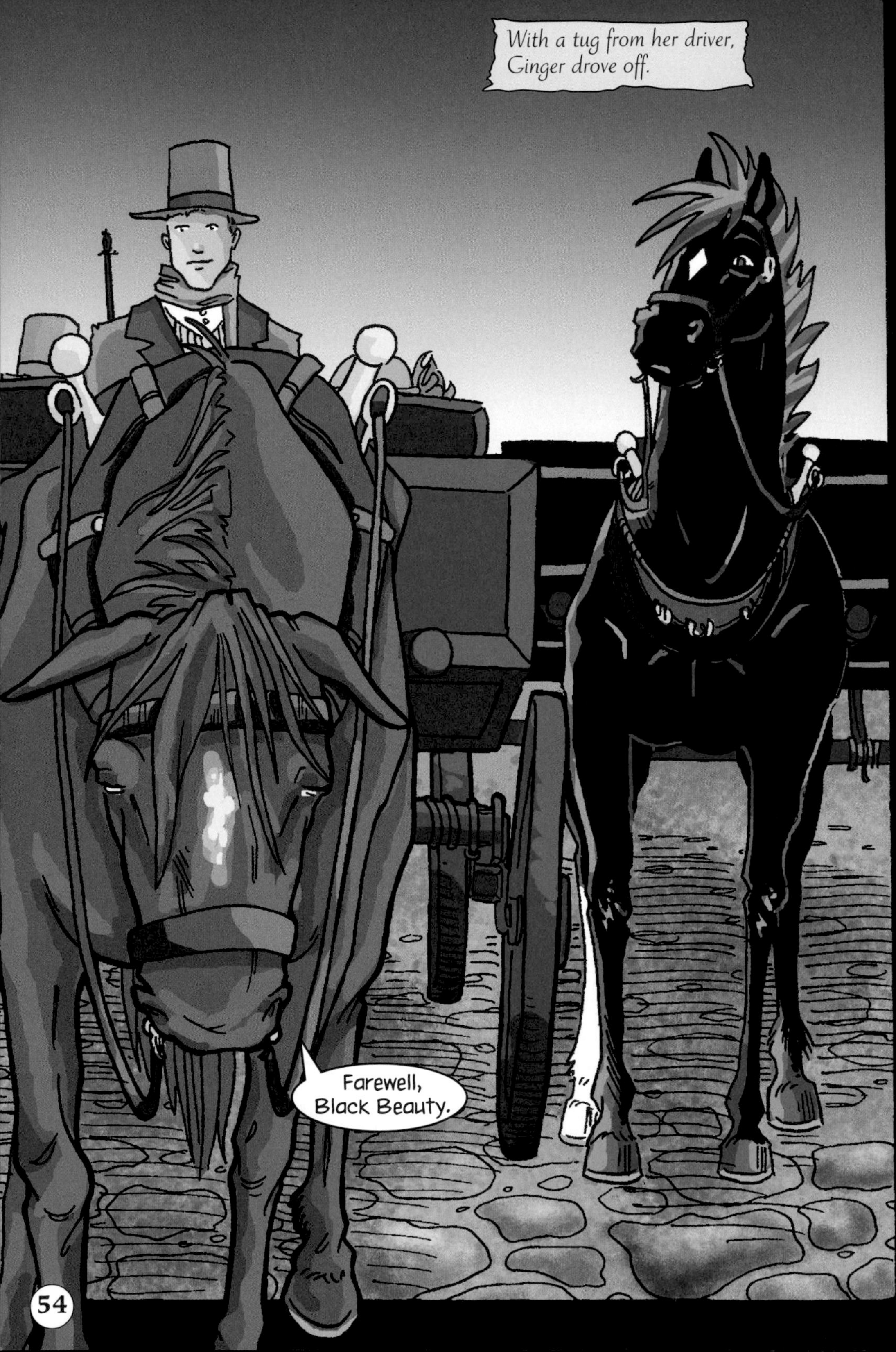
With a tug from her driver, Ginger drove off.
Farewell, Black Beauty.

A few days later, I saw a cart with a dead horse in it. I hoped it was Ginger. Then her troubles would be over.

If only men were more caring. They would shoot us instead of making us suffer so much.

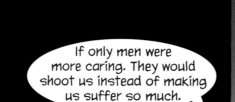

Chapter 5 ★ THE FINAL SALE

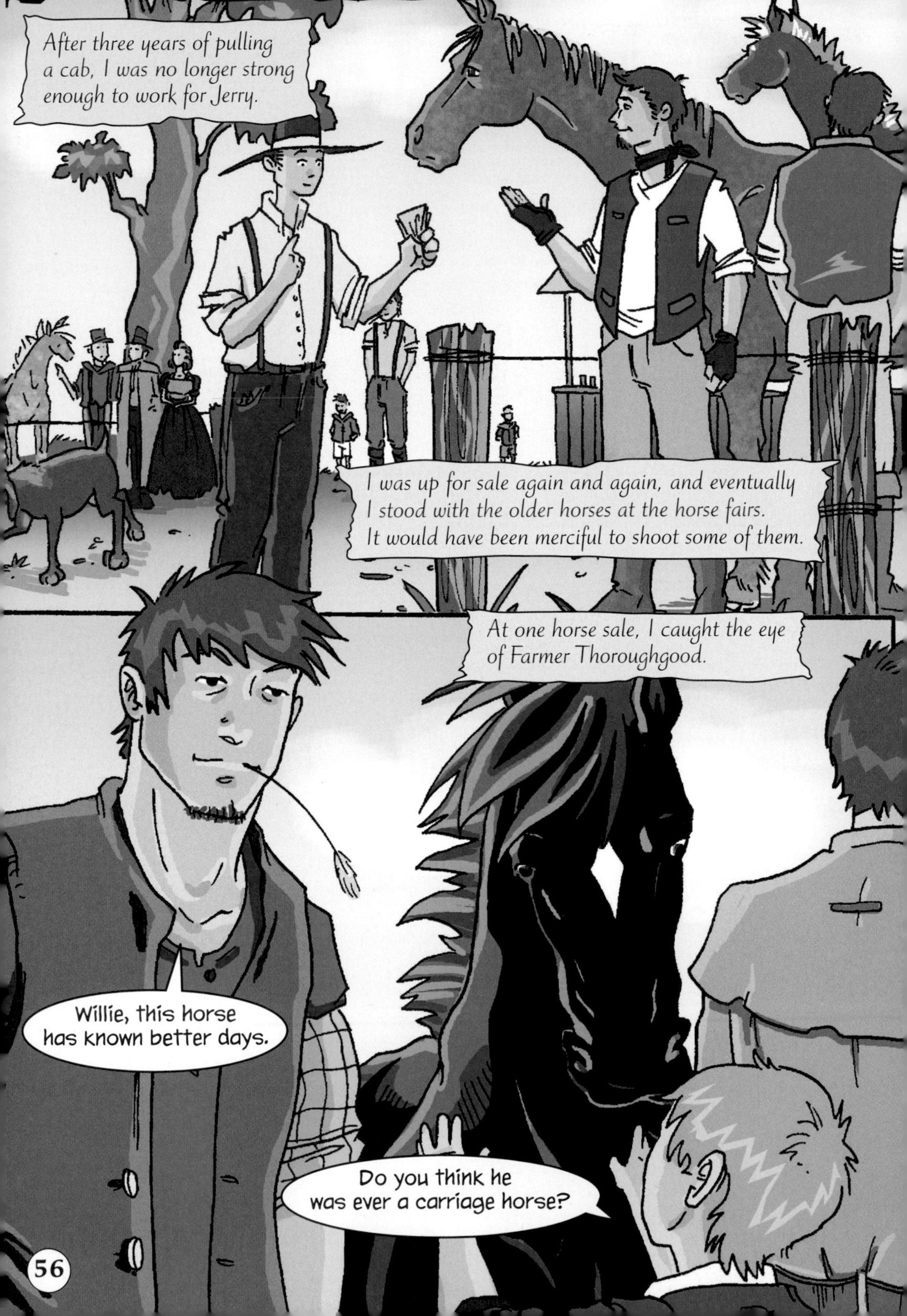
After three years of pulling a cab, I was no longer strong enough to work for Jerry.
I was up for sale again and again, and eventually I stood with the older horses at the horse fairs. It would have been merciful to shoot some of them.
At one horse sale, I caught the eye of Farmer Thoroughgood.
Willie, this horse has known better days.
Do you think he was ever a carriage horse?

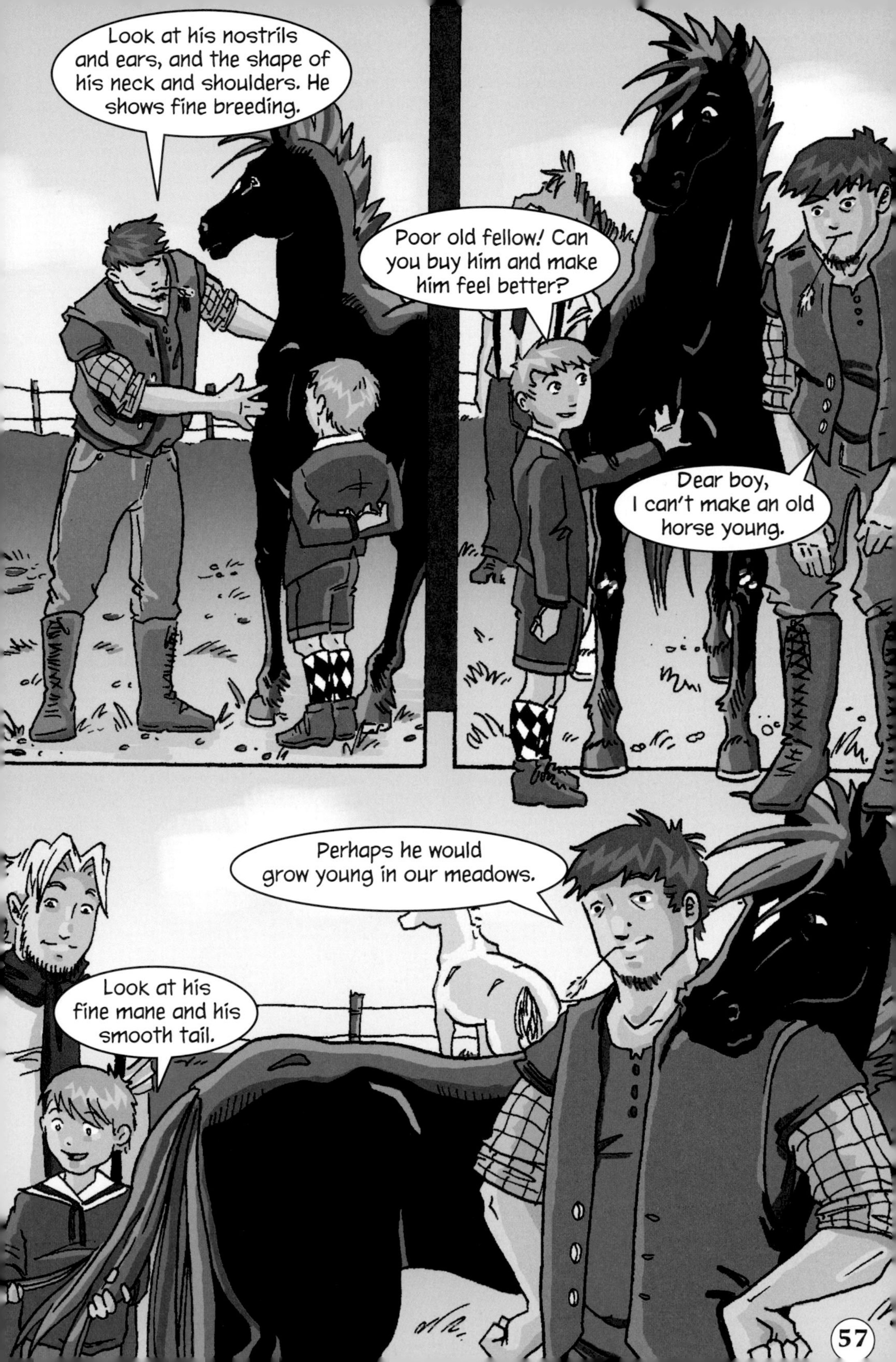
Look at his nostrils and ears, and the shape of his neck and shoulders. He shows fine breeding.
Poor old fellow! Can you buy him and make him feel better?
Dear boy, I can't make an old horse young.
Perhaps he would grow young in our meadows.
Look at his fine mane and his smooth tail.

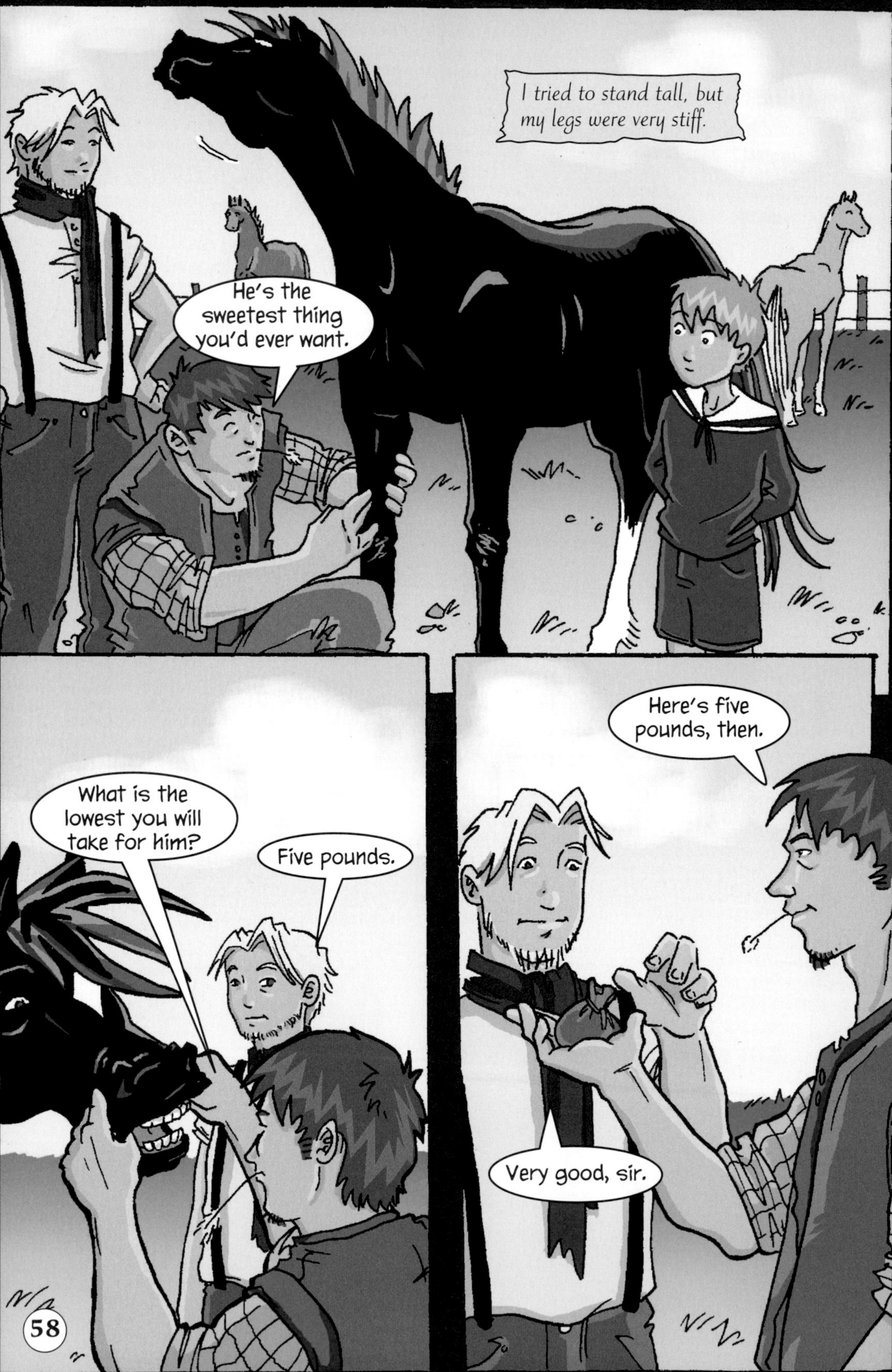
I tried to stand tall, but my legs were very stiff.
He's the sweetest thing you'd ever want.
What is the lowest you will take for him?
Five pounds.
Here's five pounds, then.
Very good, sir.

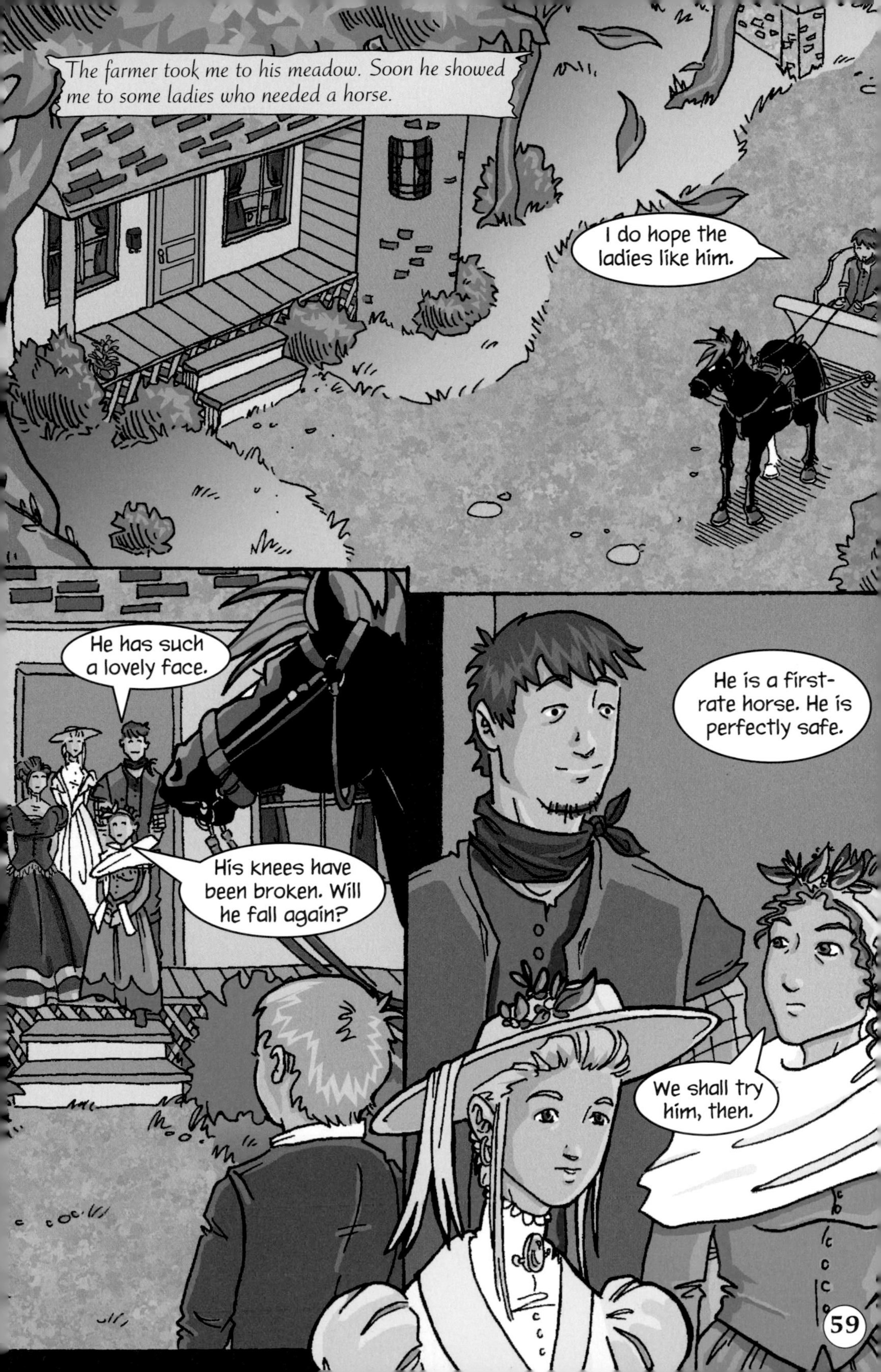
The farmer took me to his meadow. Soon he showed me to some ladies who needed a horse.
I do hope the ladies like him.
He has such a lovely face.
His knees have been broken. Will he fall again?
He is a first-rate horse. He is perfectly safe.
We shall try him, then.

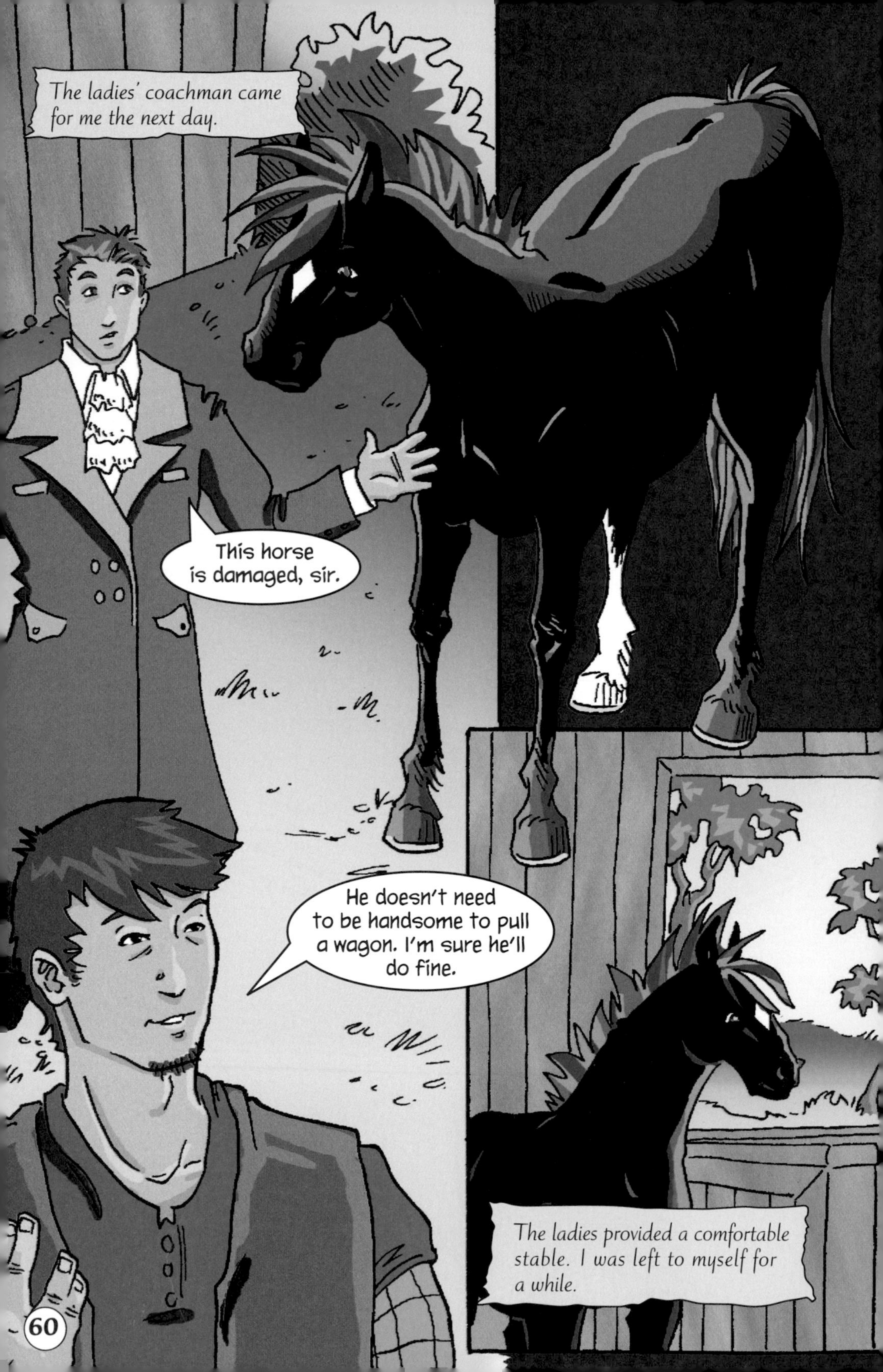

The ladies' coachman came for me the next day.
This horse is damaged, sir.
He doesn't need to be handsome to pull a wagon. I'm sure he'll do fine.
The ladies provided a comfortable stable. I was left to myself for a while.

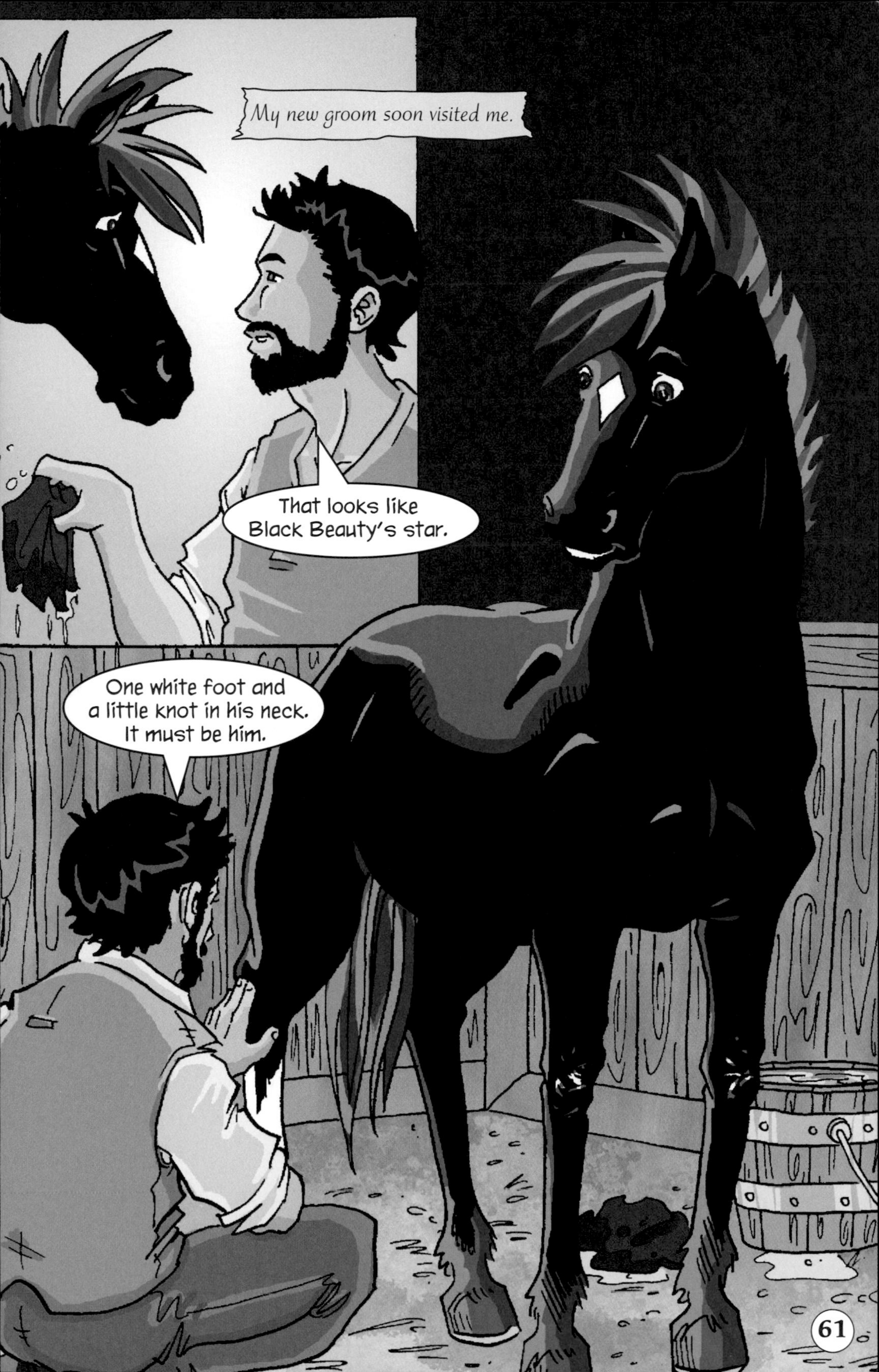
My new groom soon visited me.
That looks like Black Beauty's star.
One white foot and a little knot in his neck. It must be him.

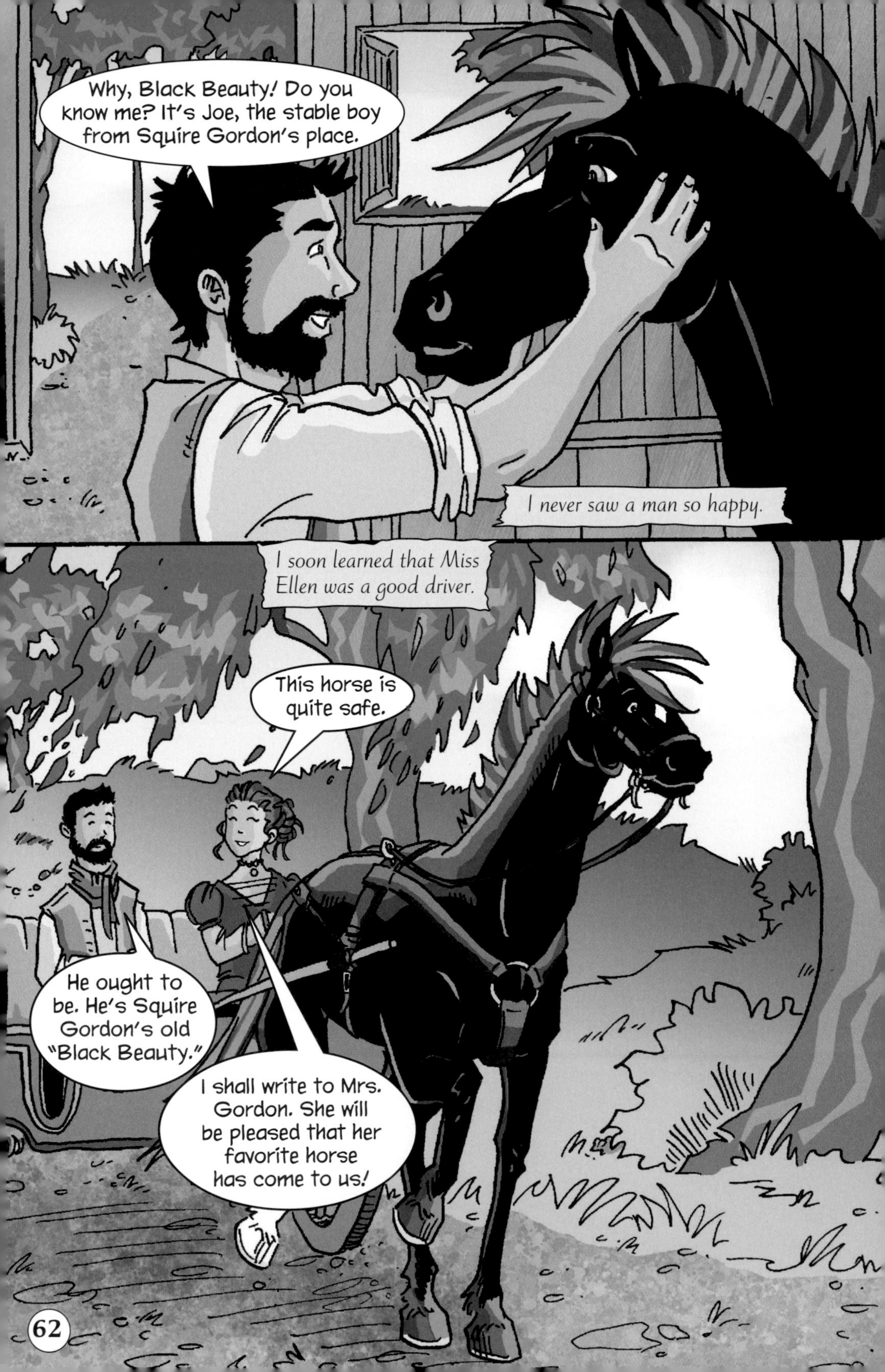
Why, Black Beauty! Do you know me? It's Joe, the stable boy from Squire Gordon's place.
I never saw a man so happy.
I soon learned that Miss Ellen was a good driver.
This horse is quite safe.
He ought to be. He's Squire Gordon's old "Black Beauty."
I shall write to Mrs. Gordon. She will be pleased that her favorite horse has come to us!

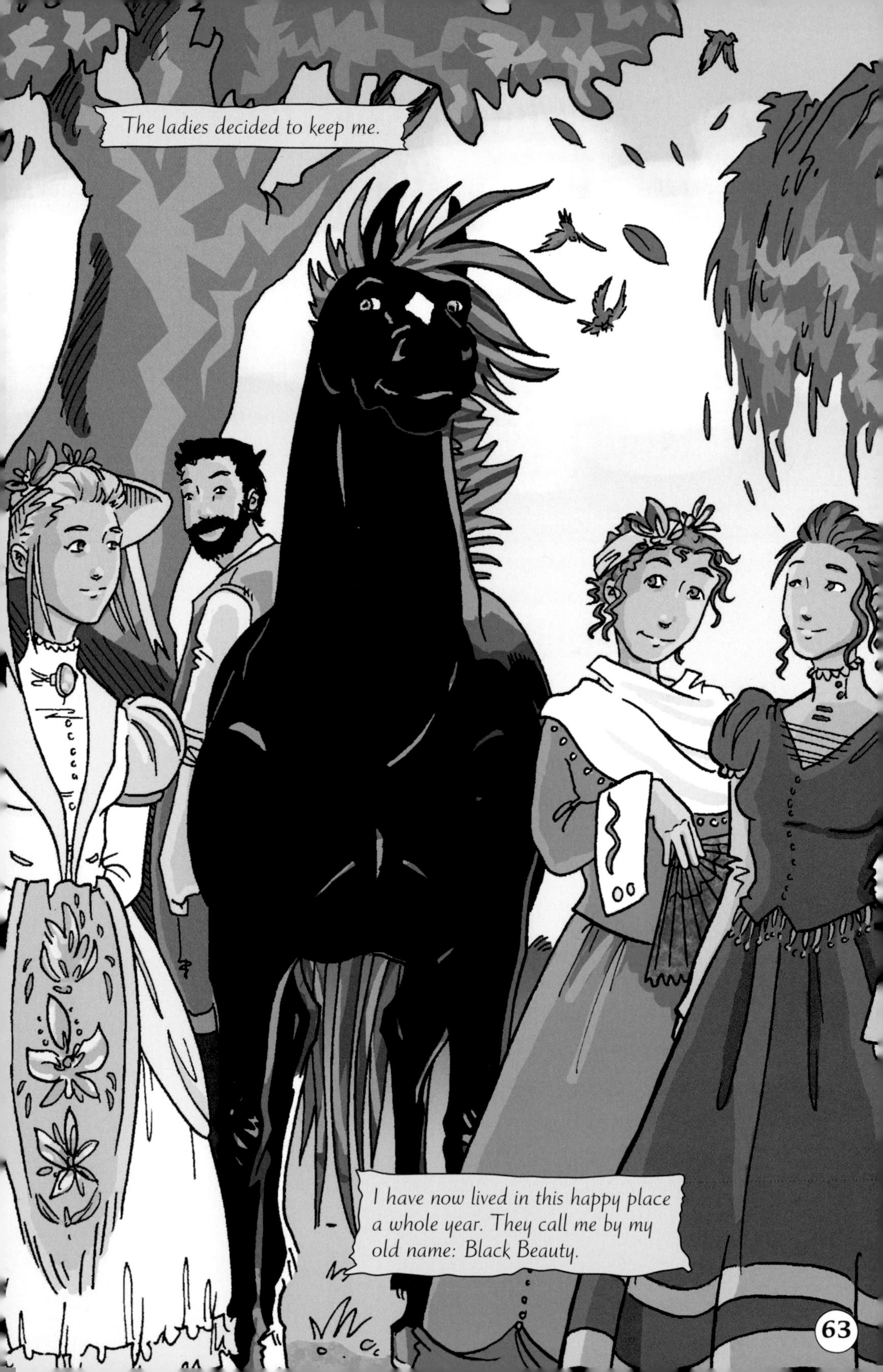
The ladies decided to keep me.
I have now lived in this happy place a whole year. They call me by my old name: Black Beauty.

ABOUT ANNA SEWELL

Anna Sewell was born in 1820 in England. Around the age of 14, Sewell fell and injured her ankles. They didn't heal properly. From then on, she had trouble walking and relied on horses to take her where she needed to go. She loved horses and was grateful for them. Sewell was shocked to see how cruelly some people treated her favorite animal.

In 1871, Sewell was told she had only a short time to live. She decided to write a book that would show the kind and loving nature of horses. That book, the only one she ever wrote, was *Black Beauty*. It has been considered a classic since it was published in 1877.

ABOUT THE AUTHOR

L. L. Owens was born in Iowa and now lives in Seattle, Washington, with her husband. She has written more than 45 books, and she enjoys visiting classrooms to talk about her writing. She likes listening to music, cooking, and exploring the Pacific Northwest.

ABOUT THE ILLUSTRATOR

When she was younger, Jennifer Tanner loved to draw humorous comics about dogs who went on spectacular adventures through time and space, meeting alien creatures along the way. Today she spends her time illustrating many comic book stories.

GLOSSARY

colts (KOLTS) — young male horses

damaged (DAM-ijd) — broken or unable to heal

Duchess (DUTCH-iss) — the name of Black Beauty's mother, who was named for a duchess, the wife of a duke

filly (FILL-ee) — a young female horse

ignore (igg-NOR) — to not notice something or pretend that something didn't happen

lord (LORD) — a person who had a royal birth or had power over others

pounds (POUNDZ) — units of money used in England

scolded (SKOLD-id) — told someone that they did something wrong, often in a mean way

squire (SKWIRE) — a country gentleman

stall (STAWL) — a section in a stable or barn where an animal is kept

The Life of a Horse in Victorian Times

Black Beauty takes place in the mid-1800s, at a time when people used horses for transportation. Cars were not yet invented, and roads were often rough dirt trails. The nicest roads were made of stones.

Horses wore **horseshoes** to protect their hooves. They usually wore a **saddle** on their backs and headgear called a **bridle**. The bridle has a **bit** that goes into the horse's mouth, and it is attached to the **reins**. The rider pulls on the reins to give signals to the horse. In the story, Black Beauty had to wear a **checkrein**. This is a short rein that keeps the horse's head high. Black Beauty also wore leather flaps called **blinders** on his bridle. They shielded his eyes, making him look straight ahead.

There are different titles for people who handle horses. The **groom** takes care of the horse in its stable. For fine carriages, which hold a few people, a **coachman** steers the horses. For a quick, short ride, people might ride in a cab. This is a small and less fancy carriage driven by a **cabbie**.

DISCUSSION QUESTIONS

1. Black Beauty's mother, Duchess, taught her son good manners. What are some good manners that you should use every day?

2. When he saw a dead horse in a cart, Black Beauty said he hoped that it was Ginger. Why did Black Beauty want Ginger to die?

3. Why did Lady York want Ginger and Black Beauty to wear the checkrein? Do you think that she treated the animals kindly?

4. At the end of the story, Black Beauty is called by his old name. Why does this make him feel happy?

WRITING PROMPTS

1. Toward the end of the story, Black Beauty thinks about Merrylegs and Ginger, his best friends. Describe each of the horses. What did they look like? How did they act?

2. Which place in the story do you think was Black Beauty's favorite? Describe your own favorite place and explain why it is your favorite.

3. Write a story about an animal in your life. What does the animal like? What does it dislike? What makes it sad or afraid? What makes it happy?

OTHER BOOKS

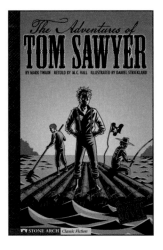

The Adventures of
TOM SAWYER
BY MARK TWAIN RETOLD BY M.C. HALL ILLUSTRATED BY DANIEL STRICKLAND
STONE ARCH Classic Fiction

THE ADVENTURES OF TOM SAWYER

Tom Sawyer is the cleverest of characters, constantly outwitting those around him. Then there is Huckleberry Finn, the envy of the town's schoolchildren because he has the rare gift of complete freedom, never attending school or answering to anyone but himself. After Tom and Huck witness a murder, they find themselves on a series of adventures that lead them to some seriously frightening situations.

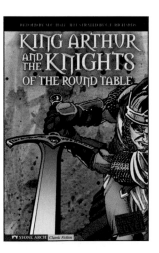

KING ARTHUR AND THE KNIGHTS OF THE ROUND TABLE
STONE ARCH Classic Fiction

KING ARTHUR AND THE KNIGHTS OF THE ROUND TABLE

In a world of wizards, giants, and dragons, King Arthur and the Knights of the Round Table are the kingdom of Camelot's only defense against the threatening forces of evil. Fighting battles and saving those in need, the Knights of the Round Table can defeat every enemy but one — themselves!

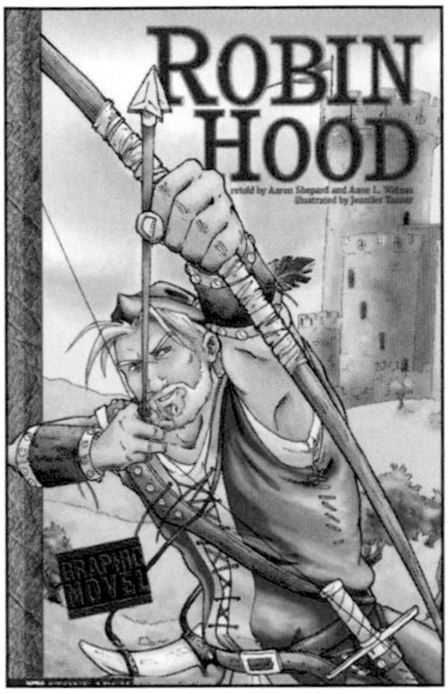
ROBIN HOOD
GRAPHIC NOVEL

ROBIN HOOD

Robin Hood and his Merrie Men are the heroes of Sherwood Forest. Taking from the rich and giving to the poor, Robin Hood and his loyal followers fight for the downtrodden and oppressed. As they outwit the cruel Sheriff of Nottingham, Robin Hood and his Merrie Men are led on a series of exciting adventures.

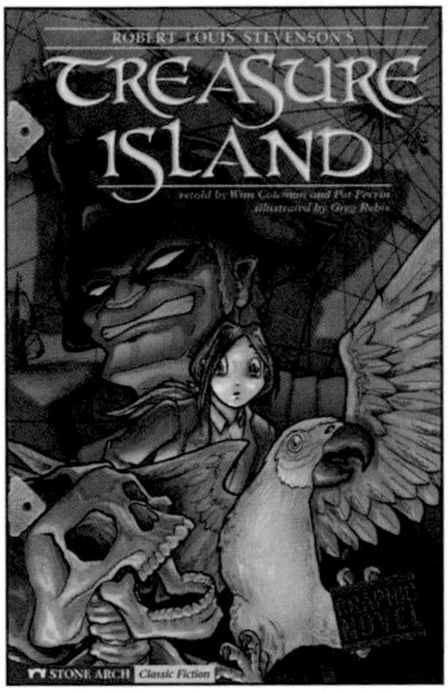
ROBERT LOUIS STEVENSON'S
TREASURE ISLAND
GRAPHIC NOVEL
STONE ARCH Classic Fiction

TREASURE ISLAND

Jim Hawkins had no idea what he was getting into when the pirate Billy Bones showed up at the doorstep of his mother's inn. When Billy dies suddenly, Jim is left to unlock his old sea chest, which reveals money, a journal, and a treasure map. Joined by a band of honorable men, Jim sets sail on a dangerous voyage to locate the loot on a faraway island. The violent sea is only one of the dangers they face. They soon encounter a band of bloodthirsty pirates determined to make the treasure their own!

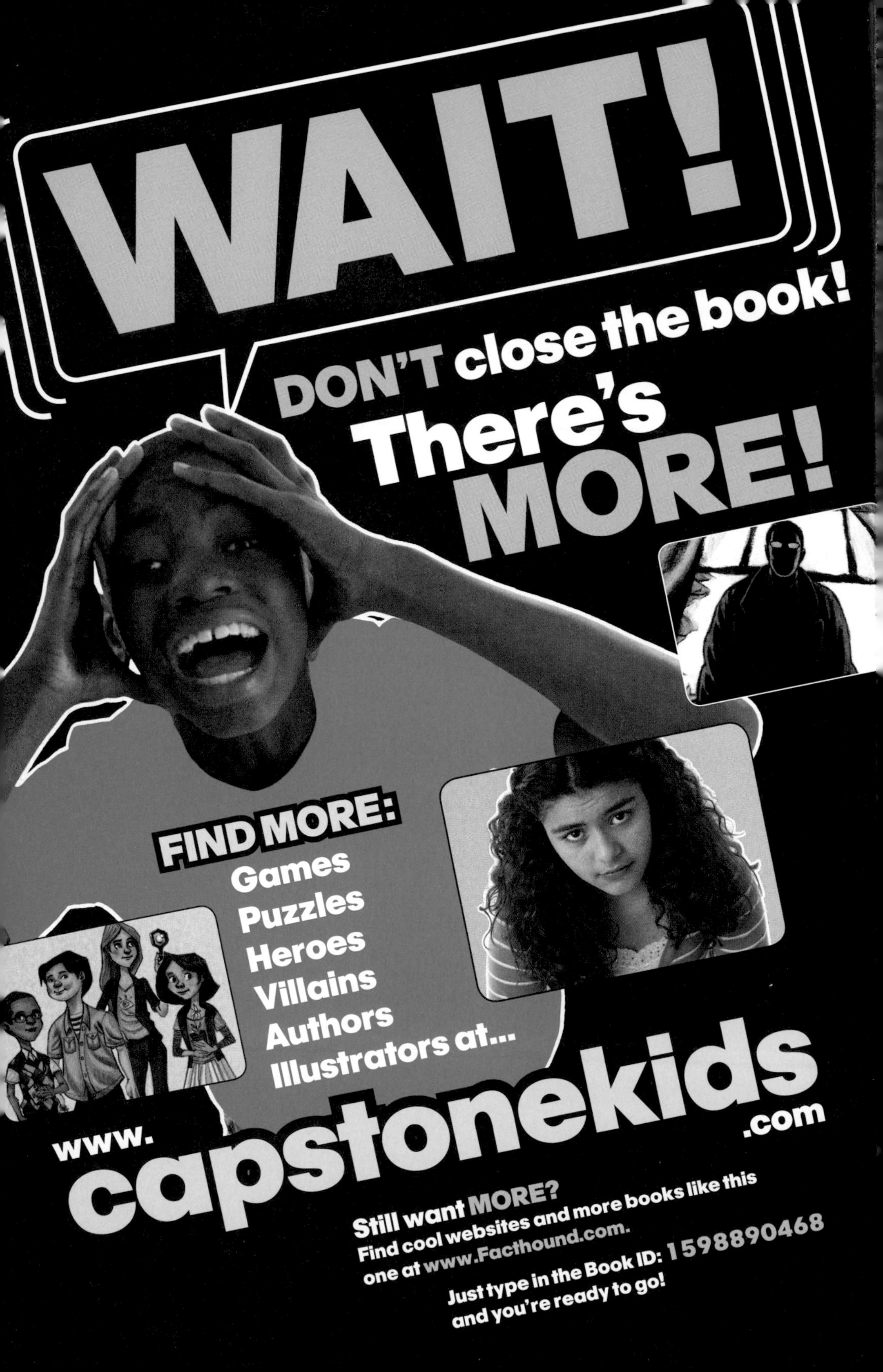
WAIT!
DON'T close the book!
There's MORE!
FIND MORE:
Games
Puzzles
Heroes
Villains
Authors
Illustrators at...
www.capstonekids.com
Still want MORE?
Find cool websites and more books like this one at www.Facthound.com.
Just type in the Book ID: 1598890468
and you're ready to go!